The Joy of Deception

The Joy of Deception

and Other Stories

Gretchen Johnson

Beaumont, Texas

ISBN: 978-0-9852552-2-0
Library of Congress Control Number: 2012934316
Manufactured in the United States of America

Cover Design: Michael Sanchez
Front Cover Photograph: Gretchen Johnson
Back Cover Photograph: Michael Vallee

Lamar University Press
Beaumont, Texas

For my parents
　　Brian and Lois Johnson
my brother
　　Alex Johnson
and my dear friends
　　Jen Nelmark and Kim Pehrson

Acknowledgments

In the writing of this book, I owe special thanks to my teachers and mentors: Joe Wenderoth, Lupe Solis, Bill Holm, Adrian Louis, Beth Weatherby, and Roger Jones.

I would also like to thank Jerry Craven and the rest of the staff of *Lamar University Press* for believing in this project and for all of their hard work.

Earlier forms of some of these stories have appeared in *Amarillo Bay* and *The Blue Bear Review*.

Contents

The Beauty of Silence

When Charlene asked me out, I went—not because I wanted to but because I never had an opportunity to say no. You see, I have never been a man of action. Instead, my life has been defined by a series of moments in which I failed to take a stand for my own preferences.

She picked the restaurant, a 1950s diner replica on the outskirts of Fargo, and even came to my house in her truck to pick me up. I sat on my old green couch watching *The Wheel of Fortune* until I heard a loud knocking on the front door. I grabbed my jacket, answered the door, and we were off.

"Can you believe this weather?" she asked, and I nodded, trying not to focus on her enormous black-rimmed glasses. "It's not supposed to be this cold yet. It's only October." She continued talking as I fastened my seatbelt.

I first met Charlene at my mother's craft store. She worked there three days a week and also held a full-time job cleaning cages at the Red River Zoo. I had never been even remotely attracted to her—her nasal voice, masculine face, ugly glasses, and frumpy body repelled me. The night of our date she wore tight jeans that were too short and left her dingy white socks exposed, a navy blue sweater, and old tennis shoes. Her long, frazzled black hair was pulled into a ponytail but still looked disheveled.

"I just couldn't believe it—those two together. She's so annoying. I don't know how he can stand it." I listened to her and reminded myself that a warm meal was coming. "And then that house they bought—it's so tiny. What will they do about children? You can't put the children in the garage."

We arrived at the restaurant, and she said, "I'm going to go relieve myself" and went to the back of the place where the bathrooms were.

"How many, sir?" the waitress asked.

"Two," I said, and she led me to a booth in the corner.

Charlene came back, wiping her wet hands on her jeans, and said, "Why are we sitting here?" I shrugged my shoulders, and she continued, "Booths are for children's birthday parties. This is a date. We need a table."

She motioned for the waitress to come over and said, "I'm sorry. The gentleman I'm with didn't know I wanted a table, so we'll be moving over here." The waitress smiled and nodded, and Charlene picked up our menus and relocated us.

I looked at the menu and visualized hamburgers, steak, and fried chicken while she talked. "Can you believe all the things that reverend does over at that church on Birch Street? He's got boys and girls spending the night at church once a month. Is everyone but me stupid enough to think they're watching movies and doing Bible studies? And then that Gayle Josephson—she threw her husband out for bowling. The man's gotta have fun, and bowling has never been associated with bad behavior. That woman should try being married to Kurt Archer. Then she would know what a bad man is made of."

The waitress came by and asked if we were ready. "Sure are," Charlene replied. "I'll have the veggie salad, and he'll have the same." I removed my finger from where it had been resting on the fried chicken dinner with mashed potatoes and looked at its description once more before shutting the menu in defeat.

"Sounds good," the waitress said and tossed her blonde ponytail behind her shoulder before picking up our menus and leaving.

"It sure does," Charlene said. "I get the salad every time. There are too many people in this world who believe the goal in life is to see who can die with the most beef in them. Do I look like someone who wishes to clog my veins with lard a little every day and then wonder why, at sixty-four, I'm in bad health? I didn't think so. I have this body and this body only. I'm not under the impression that I'll have the option to trade it in twelve years down the road."

The pretty waitress stared at Charlene from behind the counter and whispered something to her friend. They both started to laugh.

"I suppose you have to keep your sense of humor working a job like this. Not everyone has a satisfying job like selling home decorations or taking care of animals. Those animals depend on me, but who depends on these waitresses? No one. Their job is unnecessary. We could just eat somewhere else or at home," Charlene said.

I picked at a broken nail on my left hand as she kept talking. "There are a lot of people in this town I simply don't understand, people who make me question everything I learned in high school psychology. That Leonard Fellps should not be so obsessed with that dog. You'd think someone would tell him it's just a damn dog and an ugly one at that. The way he carts that thing around makes you want to just go up to him and say, 'Leonard, get yourself a woman. They at least talk to you.'"

My ears perked up, and I made a mental note to get a dog.

"What kind of a mother do you think he had that would raise a boy to spend his life living with a dog?" She took a sip of water and continued, "It does make sense, though, when you think about his mother. Loretta's a nice enough gal, but she's definitely had her share of problems. Look at Nancy, her oldest; it must be hard to raise a retarded child, knowing your drug habits ruined her life."

The waitress dropped off our plates of lettuce as I prayed for silence. Charlene took a bite and went right on, "I should take you to that zoo of mine. We have everything—camels, cows, horses, squirrels, ducks, and donkeys. You name it—it's there."

I wanted to ask about hippos.

"Granted this is North Dakota, and maybe those big city folks would degrade us by calling our zoo a petting zoo, but this is one of the most important places in the region."

She took bites of salad and chewed while talking. It was beyond unappetizing. "When I was a kid I always wanted to be a fork for Halloween. I just thought of that for some reason. Now that the holiday's coming up again, I might finally try it out for size. We're having a costume party at the zoo, and most of my co-workers will naturally come as animals, but you know me—I like to shake things up a bit, keep people in suspense. I think showing up as a fork would be really cute, and, hey, you could be the spoon. My boss would get a real kick out of that," and she chuckled with the same nasal tone and pressed onward. "The party will be two days before Halloween, so mark your calendar."

3

Throughout the rest of dinner she spoke about still more people from her church, critiqued the need for public transportation in Fargo, described in detail her morning routine, and confessed to a weird obsession with sheep.

She took me home after forcing me to pay for the food I didn't even want by sliding the bill over to my side of the table after the waitress had placed it directly in the middle.

I assumed she would drop me off, all the while talking endlessly, and drive off into the night, leaving me to question if we did actually go on a date, but I wasn't lucky enough for that outcome. She instead followed me into my house and said, "Give me a tour. I want to see every inch of this place."

I stood alone in my living room while she scurried about the house shouting things like, "interesting bed spread," "cute little table," and "you're a briefs kind of guy? I should've known." I just stood there stunned until she returned. "You look so formal. Sit down," she ordered, so I sat down on the edge of the couch. "This evening could've been a lot better, you know. Flowers would have been a nice touch. You're a nice guy and all, but a girl needs excitement, and a girl needs romance—two things I'm not sure you're capable of giving me."

I wanted her to leave, to stop talking and just go. She stayed.

"I think you would be a Pookie. I know it's far too early in the game to give each other pet names, but I think Pookie fits you." She grabbed my hand. "You've got that kind of nerdy cute appeal to you."

I touched my kneecap, struggling to find any sign of masculinity.

"Oh, what the hell . . . maybe we should. Maybe pet names are okay at first and shouldn't be left as a desperate attempt to spice things up when the relationship is worn in."

I wondered what she meant by *relationship*.

"Pookie, I think your mom will definitely approve of us. What do you think?" She grabbed my neck aggressively and wrapped her pale, flabby arms around it, pulling my head into her small chest.

She looked down at me and said, "I think a kiss would be appropriate at this juncture. Don't you?"

Before I could answer, she kissed me. It was awful—dry, short, and

4

forced.

She stood up and said, "Thanks for dinner. I can't wait to see you again," and, just like that, she was gone. I watched through the window as she got into her truck and drove away. I went back to the couch, put my feet on the coffee table, and the beauty of silence surrounded me.

Snow Storm

I held my door open while she drove to make sure we were still on the road.

"I told you we should have left earlier. The weather report said this was coming. I told you. Why don't you ever listen to me?" I asked.

"We're fine. I'm only going five miles an hour. Nothing's going to happen. We're fine. Trust me; I have lived out here my whole life. This is nothing," Kristin said. We had already been driving for about an hour, and the storm was gaining strength as the snow accumulated on the deserted highway and the wind lifted up snow from previous storms and redistributed it in the air around us.

"Nothing?" I shouted. "We can't see anything! It's two in the morning, there is a guy passed out in the back seat, it's going to take three hours to get the fifteen miles back to Marshall, and we might die."

"We probably won't die," she said. "This is not nearly as bad as the blizzard of eighty-nine when my dad's truck was stuck in the ditch for four days, and he had to eat the dog food in the backseat to survive."

"Why are you telling me this now?" I asked while keeping my eyes on the strip of pavement that appeared every few seconds when the wind picked up and momentarily swept the snow away.

"I said it's not as bad as that storm," she said.

"It better not be because we don't have the bag of dog food, so we'll starve," I said.

"There is nothing to worry about."

"Then why do students freeze to death every semester in situations just like this?" I asked.

"Because they're stupid city kids, no offense, and leave their cars to try to find a building."

"How can you bring up the city versus country thing now? You're the one from here, and it was your stupid idea to stay at the party. I'm the city kid, and I knew we should have left hours ago," I said.

"But things were going so well with Cletus," she said.

"So well? He's only interested in you after eight beers, and he is only with us to get a ride back to Marshall. We're risking our lives out here for nothing. He won't even remember this in the morning."

"You just don't understand how these things work," she said.

"I don't understand? Really? How long have I been dating Justin? How many one night stands did you have last year?"

"That's not the point," she said.

"Didn't you notice that Cletus was talking to Hillary most of the night?"

"Yeah, but he was talking to me for the last two hours," she said.

"That's because Hillary was smart enough to leave the party before the storm came in."

"I doubt the storm had anything to do with her leaving. She didn't seem to be having a good time," she said.

Just then the car hit a patch of black ice and skated uncontrollably on the road. I closed the door and held my breath while Kristin steered out of it. I opened the door again and determined that somehow we were still on the road. Cletus grunted and shifted his position in the backseat. "I am never going to an out of town party again. Don't even bother asking," I said.

"We can always stay there next time."

"And stay in a house with eight guys out in the middle of no where? No thanks. I think I'd rather be out here," I said.

"You are totally overreacting," she said.

A strong gust hit us, making the road a couple of feet beyond my door momentarily visible. "I see the ditch. Move the car over a little," I said, and she slowly steered to the left.

The wind was intensifying, and even Kristin's Buick with its solid body and sturdy features could no longer be called a good winter car. With every gust, the storm shoved the car to the right, and I watched Kristin's hands tighten on the steering wheel as we fought our way back to the center of the road. "What happens if another car is on the road? I can't even tell what lane we're in," I said.

"I don't think anyone else would be out in this," she said.

"But what if..."

"Then we'll probably hit the car head-on, but we're only driving about as fast as someone walking, and the other car would be doing the same, so nothing would really happen. It would be the same effect of accidentally backing into a car while parallel parking. No big deal."

I didn't understand how she could be so calm. I worried about everything. Justin and I had been dating for two years, but we didn't even have sex. I was too worried about getting pregnant and ruining my plan to become a lawyer by twenty-four. My doctor chuckled when I told her that even the statistical improbability of getting pregnant while on two forms of birth control could not sway me. Kristin, on the other hand, never seemed concerned about the possible results of sex. She frequently slept with guys she met at parties, men she met at her grocery store job, and even once with a guy she met at the adjoining gas pump. More than that, she didn't always make the guys wear condoms, and she usually shrugged her shoulders with a smirk on her face during my frequent lectures about this.

"Don't you have a test in the morning?" I asked.

"Yeah, it should be easy. I'm not too worried."

"Did you study?"

"A little. It'll be fine. If I fail the class, I can always take it again," she said. I took my left hand off the door to turn the heater up a notch. "It's warm enough," she said and turned it back down.

"That's because you're not the one sitting by the open door," I said.

"You need to relax," she said.

"You said that this afternoon when you convinced me to come to the party, and look what relaxing got me. Half my body is freezing, and I'm worried that I'll never sleep in my bed again." I looked over my shoulder. Cletus was sprawled out across the backseat, using his jacket for a pillow and not wearing his seatbelt. "How is he sleeping through this?"

"I wish you were," she said. "I would much rather be talking to him."

"Yeah, I'm sure he'd be a real treat after drinking half the alcohol supply of the Cottonwood liquor store," I said.

"You really need to give people a chance. Not everyone can be as boring as you and Justin."

The truth is that I liked boring. Boring was easy. Boring was safe. Kristin was always trying to convince me to veer away from boring, as though it were like taking a vacation to Florida, but her version of excitement was danger. I looked over at her a few times during that drive home and noticed that, as we shouted back and forth to each other, she seemed to be almost smiling.

It was nearly three a.m., and I glanced over at the gas gauge for the first time. "Do you realize that you're almost out of gas?" I asked.

"I have almost a fourth of a tank. I can go a hundred miles on that."

"First of all, you can't, and second of all, why would you go to a party out of town without a full tank of gas?"

"It's only twenty miles out of Marshall," she said.

"What if something happened?"

"Something did happen," she said.

"Exactly!" I shouted.

"And we're fine. We'll get to Marshall soon. I promise. Do you want me to drive a little faster?"

"No!"

"You know you would think this was beautiful if you were in your room," she said. "You always talk about how great the blizzards are out here, how they're way better than even St. Paul's famous Halloween blizzard of ninety-one."

"I'm not in my dorm room. I'm trapped in a moving automobile. It's not beautiful. It's terrifying."

"See it how you want," she said. "But you and I both know this is going to be a great story at the dining hall tomorrow." Suddenly the car struck something and squashed it under the wheel as we felt the car shake.

"What was that?" I yelled.

"Probably just a squirrel or a small dog," she said and started laughing.

"Why are you laughing? This is horrible."

"Come on, Paige. Don't you think it's a little funny? Cletus is still asleep." She looked at me.

"Just keep your eyes on the road," I said.

"I can't see the road. You're the one watching the road," she said.

I remembered learning once that white is not the absence of color; it is, in fact, the presence of all colors. Black is the absence of color, but that night it seemed that the opposite was true as I sat in the car and looked out into the nothingness the snow created. On a black night, you could turn your headlights on and see the colors of the world, know where the road curved up ahead, see the trees and houses and mailboxes, and find your way home. But on a white night, the snow saturated the world and stole your ability to see the landscape's various shades. It made you blind as you drove through the emptiness of a colorless sky. The world wasn't dark that night; it was flooded with white.

"I'll take you out for Chinese buffet tomorrow. It'll be fun," she said, and I wondered what the chances were of being infected with food poisoning.

"We'll see," I said.

"How am I doing?"

"It seems okay. Maybe move to the left a bit," I said, and she slid the car over about a foot.

"Don't you think he's cute sleeping back there?"

"No. He's annoying. What happened to the idea of a guy protecting women in dangerous situations?"

"Give him a break. He had too much to drink," she said.

"Yeah, that's a common thread in history books and great romances. We've all heard countless stories where the handsome man sleeps off a night of binge drinking while the women rescue themselves."

"What could he really do anyway?" she asked.

"That's not the point. Why do you always sleep with these guys? He doesn't even know your name."

"I'm pretty sure that's not true," she said. Just then my slightly open door hit a pole, bending my hand back at an awkward angle. I screamed, and she said, "What was that?"

"Stop the car. We hit something." She stopped, and I got out, wiped the snow off the green sign and saw, *Marshall, 2 miles*. We were almost home. I couldn't see the town lights like I could on a clear day, but for a moment, standing there outside of the car and feeling the flakes hit my face, it almost looked beautiful.

I got back in the car. "Well?" she said.

"We're two miles out of town," I said.

"See. I told you we would get there."

"We're not there yet," I said.

"We will be."

I sat silent and pictured my flannel snowman pajamas. They were waiting for me, draped over my desk chair, warm from the heating vent on the neighboring wall. We didn't talk much the rest of the way but instead concentrated on everything going on outside of the car and inside too: the deep song of the wind rushing across the fields, the muffled sound of Cletus snoring in the backseat, the red line on the gasoline gauge that pointed closer and closer to empty, the unsteady feeling of driving above the road on a slippery surface of snow and ice, and the fear of moving through a place we could not see.

I reminded myself that as soon as we got into town we would see the world again. Buildings and trees would cut the wind and slow the stirring of snow. Visibility would not be great, but it would exist, and we would see the street and find our way home.

The Buick lumbered on, and I gave directions to keep Kristin on the road. Those last two miles, I sometimes took my glove off and leaned out of the car to dig my fingers down and feel the street beneath the snow. We were moving so slowly that the friction didn't hurt, and my seatbelt held me in as I felt the wind slip down the back of my neck.

"Holy shit! Where am I?" Cletus' voice in the backseat startled me, so I quickly sat back up and closed the door.

"We're almost back," Kristin said.

"Back where?" he asked.

"To Marshall," she said.

"Why are we going so slow?" he asked.

"Oh, my God!" I shouted at him. "We're in the middle of a white-out blizzard. We've been driving in this for two hours while you slept in the backseat."

"Really?" he said.

"Yes, really. You met Kristin at the party and wanted a ride home."

"Which one of you is Kristin?" he asked.

"That's me," Kristin said and smiled at him over her shoulder.

"Cool," he said and rested his head against the backseat.

"I'm in your philosophy . . ." she started to say, but the car slammed into something and stopped moving.

"Holy shit!" Cletus said.

"Are you okay?" I asked Kristin.

"Yeah. I wonder what that was," she said.

I got out of the car and found the problem. The gate that usually stood open by the highway at the edge of town had been closed and chained. A huge orange sign in the middle read *Road Closed*. I got back in the car and said, "The highway patrol must have barricaded the road when the storm started."

"That would explain why we didn't meet any other cars," Kristin said and laughed.

"You think this is funny? What are we going to do now?" I asked.

"It's no big deal. We'll just leave the car here and walk back to the dorms. It's less than a mile." I couldn't believe she was so calm about leaving her car, but there really weren't any other options.

"Do you think the car will be okay?" I asked.

"Sure. I'll lock it and come back for it before class in the morning. Cletus will give me a ride, right?"

He hesitated and mumbled that he would, and we all got out of the car and started walking home. It wasn't very cold. The overnight low was around twenty, and trudging through the deep snow was difficult, so it didn't take long for me to start sweating under my bulky winter jacket. I walked ahead, eager to get back to my room and get some sleep before my alarm went off a few hours later. Cletus and Kristin walked leisurely, and they talked about the party, Kristin filling Cletus in on all the details he missed at the end of the night when he was too drunk to comprehend the events. I thought about our drive back to Marshall. Maybe Kristin was right; it was kind of funny.

13

The three of us walked on empty streets while the rest of the town slept in the safety of their houses. As we got close enough to see the tall brick dorm buildings peeking through the haze of snow, I no longer felt the sting of wet socks against my skin, and the blizzard became beautiful as I knew for sure that I would soon be in my bed and separated from the white wilderness of the previous hours.

We got to my dorm first, and I rushed upstairs to the comfort of my room. I watched from my fourth floor window as Kristin and Cletus walked past my building and were soon obscured by the snow between us.

I lay in bed that night hoping that Cletus was wearing a condom, wondering if I should call Kristin in the morning to make sure she was awake for her test, and trying to remember if she locked the car before we left it at the edge of town. I had somehow made it home that night, and I knew that I wouldn't be in the car the next time a storm came in, but I also knew that Kristin would. I tucked the blankets tightly under me and wondered how many more storms there would be before Kristin didn't make it home.

Life in a Vacuum

Paul reluctantly slid out of the full-sized bed quietly so as not to wake his wife, Stacy. It was another Tuesday morning just like the one last week and the one before that and actually a lot like the rest of the days of the week. Paul felt the weight of his life and all the mundane responsibilities pushing him down, but he somehow always managed to move forward.

Upon reaching the bathroom and looking into the blurry mirror that should have been cleaned months ago, he tucked the loose hairs behind his ears and ran the water to brush his teeth. Stacy was constantly talking about saving money by conserving the use of water and electricity, so Paul agreed that he would only shower once every three days. This was not one of those fortunate days. He wet down his old toothbrush quickly, turned off the water, applied a small amount of generic toothpaste, brushed, and rinsed off the frazzled toothbrush.

"Didn't I tell you to wake me up before you leave for work?" Stacy said. He hadn't heard her footsteps, but suddenly she was standing in the bathroom doorway, looking awful in her old yellow nightshirt.

"I haven't left yet," he said.

"Don't you be sarcastic to me," she said.

"I was only . . ."

"Don't talk back," she said and poked her head into the bathroom, inspecting the space and searching for a mistake. "I told you not to let our toothbrushes touch. My God! How many times do I have to repeat the same damn things before you hear them? It's completely unsanitary for something that you scrub your mouth with to touch my toothbrush."

Paul quickly moved his toothbrush to the other side of the glass and made sure the bristles were facing away from Stacy's.

"And when I said to wake me up before you leave I wasn't talking about the second before you walk out the door. Don't you want to spend some time with your wife and talk in the morning before going to work all day?"

He stood there looking at the old tile floor and said, "I was only trying to let you sleep a little more."

"Sleep is a waste of time," she said and headed to the closet to pick out her work clothes.

Paul turned on the water and let it run while he combed his hair. He knew it would irritate her, and this thrilled him a little. Stacy dressed quickly, and he heard the closet door close, a warning that she was coming. He turned the water off.

Stacy appeared again, this time wearing a blue dress with huge white and pink flowers stretched across the fabric that made her body even larger and lumpier than it normally appeared. "Where are you working today?" she asked.

"Georgia's Diner," he said.

"Make sure you come home right after work."

"I will."

"And don't buy anything today. With all the damn gum you buy we could be saving that money for retirement. You're chewing us into poverty."

Stacy accounted for every penny Paul spent. He had to provide receipts for every purchase, and even taking cash out of the account didn't give him any freedom because she even demanded to know how that was spent, and she meticulously kept records to make sure that no money was missing. Paul started to wonder how much trouble a person would get into for stealing a pack of gum.

"Are you listening?" she said.

"Yes. I got it. Spend no money," he said.

Paul's life had inevitably become exactly what everyone predicted it would be—a chore barely worth doing. He had never been an attractive guy with his awkward features and short, stout body, so people tended to expect little from him, and he became that expectation. He had married Stacy because she was the first girl who ever took the time to talk to him, and he feared she would be the last. He didn't want to give up his one chance if that's what it turned out to be. She was never a pretty thing to look at. Plain would be a complimentary word to describe her appearance. She didn't even look good on their wedding day, and he hated her for that. He had thought any girl could be marginally pretty in a wedding dress, but with her tired looking and uneven eyes, low cheekbones, and severe under-bite, Stacy was only herself in a fancy dress escorting her.

"I'm taking off. See you tonight," he said while grabbing a tattered leather jacket.

"Okay then," she half yelled with the usual whiny voice.

Paul and Stacy never kissed—not to say goodbye or for any other reason. It seemed like too much effort to put into such an uninteresting scenario.

Paul got into his old green truck and drove to the diner four miles out of town to do what he always did, clean the carpet. He had taken the job when he moved to Deer Park because it was the only one available that required no previous experience. That was twelve years ago. Every day he drove to his assigned location and cleaned the carpet. Sometimes it was a private residence, but more often he cleaned for businesses.

The diner was basically empty since it was only six in the morning. He greeted the waitress, explained why he was there, and got to work. A young girl and boy sat at a table drinking orange juice and eating pancakes, probably a high school couple getting breakfast before school. They were holding hands while they ate and making do with their spare hand. It annoyed Paul.

He focused his attention on the machine and watched as the dark blue carpet slowly turned to its intended shade of a lighter hue as the machine pulled out the dirt. This was the sole achievement he could claim, the transformation of dirty to clean in something as trivial as carpet, but he accepted this because he realized it was the best he could have. Things weren't going to get any better. Sometimes, when his wife yelled at him in public, he stared hard at the carpet and imagined himself making it better. His mind removed the filth of life, and, for a moment, he couldn't hear her anymore.

The Joy of Deception

I watched my breath fog up the windshield as I drove down Main Avenue toward Reed's apartment. He pulled at a loose thread in his glove, stared out the window at the deserted snow-lined streets, and wasn't talkative for most of the drive. This behavior seemed strange given his typical personality as well as the subtle shift in seasons happening around us. March evenings in Fargo were still cold, but daytime temperatures were starting to settle a few degrees above freezing and seemed to make the local inhabitants more animated after enduring what felt like endless months of winter.

Spending Thursday evenings at Coaches Sports Bar with Reed was becoming a routine for us. It was something I looked forward to, something I counted on.

"I'm going to miss hanging out with you when I'm gone," Reed said.

"So you did decide to move to Sioux Falls?" I asked.

"Nope," he said and rolled his window down, a habit I had become used to. He often said he liked the feeling of cold wind competing with the warm sensation of alcohol in his veins.

"So you're moving somewhere else?" I asked.

"Not exactly somewhere."

"What are you talking about?"

"I'll tell you later."

I took a right onto 12th Avenue and pulled my hat down over my ears to block out the cold North Dakota air. Reed extended his hand out of the open window and hummed a song I had never heard.

"Are you going to come in?" he asked as I pulled into his parking lot.

"I suppose I could for a while," I said.

19

Reed moved to Fargo to be near his girlfriend, Sara, but she broke things off the day after he arrived for reasons he wished not to disclose. It had been a month since then, and, with no real reason to live in Fargo, he spent his days sleeping until four in the afternoon and his nights at the bar watching people and pretending to be a part of their easy happiness.

His apartment was a place of comfort for me, an escape from planning a wedding, selling shoes, and attending school. He had everything organized the same way he had in his apartment in Marshall, a town four hours south where I had first met him in college, and being there made me feel that I was home again. He lived his life the way children believed adulthood would look. He sometimes had a fort of couch cushions and sheets set up in the living room; he usually bought blue and green light bulbs because he preferred their ambiance to the stark white ones, and he replaced the mini-blinds that came with the apartment with moon and star curtains. I didn't want him to move. When he came to Fargo, I felt I had a piece of my old life back again, and I wasn't ready to give that up yet.

"So what were you talking about in my car?" I asked as he sat down on the floor to take off his brown boots.

"It doesn't matter," he said in a defeated tone.

"Yes it does. You can tell me anything. You know that. We've been friends for three years."

He tugged at the hole forming in his jeans and said, "I have a heart problem."

"What kind of a heart problem?" I asked.

"The kind that they can't fix."

"What do you mean? What's wrong?"

"My heart skips beats sometimes, and it's doing it more and more often. I went to the Mayo Clinic in November, and they said I probably wouldn't live to see the first of January."

"What? How long have you known about this?"

"I found out when I was eighteen." He was twenty-seven.

"And you never told me?"

"I haven't told many people. I didn't want them to feel sorry for me."

"But I'm your friend, and I would want to know so I could be there for you in any way I can. Does anyone else know about this?"

"I told Julie and Alexis but no one else," he said and walked into his room to put on a Norah Jones CD.

"Why are you here then and not with your family?" I asked, wondering if he was making up a medical condition as a desperate attempt for attention. In college, he was known for his storytelling, but such a significant lie seemed inconceivable.

"It's easier here. When I'm around them I'm more aware of it, but when I'm here my life still feels normal."

I followed him and sat on his bed. I sank into the feather-filled mattress and watched his hands move nervously through his strawberry blonde hair as he sat on the floor and leaned against the bed frame. "Are you being serious about all this?" I asked, knowing he was drunk.

"I wouldn't make up something like this. I'm just so sick of being sick. I hate being tired all the time," he said and put his face in his hands.

"What can I do for you?"

"There's really nothing you can do."

"I'm here for you all the time. You know that, right? You can call me whenever you need to talk or just need a hug, five a.m. or in the middle of the day. I'm here."

"That's why I drink so much," he said. "It doesn't hurt as much when I drink."

"Are you in any pain right now?" I asked, guessing he had consumed at least eight beers that night.

"Not right now. It comes and goes. I don't want to talk about this anymore. I hate talking about it," he said and turned to me.

Not knowing what to say, I replied, "Okay. So what are you doing tomorrow? Do you want to go out for coffee?"

"I don't know."

"You don't know?"

He lay down on the floor and picked at the carpet with his long fingers while Norah Jones sang, "Summer days have gone too soon. You shoot the moon and miss completely," and I thought about the summer day when Reed and I had driven to Long Creek and spent the afternoon eating Chinese food and ice cream and watching movies at his parents' house. "I don't think we should hang out anymore," he said and buried his head in his arms.

"What? Why?"

He looked up at me and said, "It's just not a good idea."

"What are you talking about? I'm going to be supportive of you. I am not going to stop being your friend right now."

"It's not about my health problem," he said.

"It's not?"

"Nope."

"Then what?" I asked and sat down on the floor beside him. "Come on, you can tell me anything."

His breathing got heavy, and he pushed his feet into the thick brown carpet but said nothing.

"Reed, please tell me."

"I'm sorry . . . I'm attracted to you. I can't be around you and watch you plan your wedding with someone else."

"What? You're not attracted to me. You're just drunk right now."

"I'm sorry, but I am attracted to you. I have been for a long time. I think my heart condition is just making me more honest with people."

"Don't be sorry, but this isn't good," I said.

"I know. I love hanging out with you, but I don't think it's a good idea anymore. When I called your house in the Cities over Christmas break and you told me that you had gotten engaged, I felt my stomach drop, and I wanted to hang up the phone right then."

"Is that why you didn't seem very excited for me? I was wondering about that."

"I've wanted to be with you since the first semester I knew you, but you always had a boyfriend." He stared right at me.

"Reed?"

"What?"

"Tell me the truth. Are you just saying all of this because you're drunk and bored with your life here?"

"I promise I'm telling the truth. The alcohol just gave me the courage to say what I've been hiding from you for a long time," he said.

I bit the bottom of my lip before I spoke, knowing that I was about to step into dangerous territory, but I was bored with what my life had become. My fiancé offered me safety and stability, a path with predictable scenery, but, as I looked around Reed's room, I knew I wanted something else. The soft glow from the blue light bulb and the intense thrill of never knowing what he was going to say next persuaded me to say, "I've always wanted to be with you too." Snapshots of moments when I had sat beside him and fought off the urge to kiss him passed through me. "Look at me."

He pulled his head up and said, "Are you serious?"

"I wish I wasn't because this complicates everything so much that it's hard to even think about it, but Lynn was always my second choice. You were my first, but I thought you always looked at me like a friend."

"Ada, I love you. I've loved you since the first semester I knew you. I remember seeing you in those overalls, looking at that long red hair . . . and thinking that I could spend the rest of my life with you. I want us to be that old married couple walking in the park and for people to ask, 'who is that cute couple?' I want to . . ."

"Okay, slow down," I said, trying to remember if I had ever worn overalls to class. "I'm engaged to Lynn. Remember? I'm gonna have to take a lot of time to think about everything. These are not the kind of decisions that I can make in an instant."

"I know, so what should we do?" he asked.

"I don't know," I said and felt patches of sweat forming on my skin.

The year before, in college, Reed was known for the mysterious ways he could seduce women. He had roughly half of the characteristics women typically find attractive. He was a few inches over six feet, had strong yet gentle looking hands, and had eyes that were expressive enough to convince women of the genuineness of what he was saying, but he had awkward features too. His upper lip jutted out a little more than normal, and he had so many freckles that they connected in some places and almost overshadowed the pale pigment of his skin tone. It was his voice, though, that held the ability to win over almost anyone. It was deep like a narrator on a documentary but had the accent of a Midwestern farmer. This created the unique combination of sexiness and simplicity that made women believe he was as fascinating as an actor but also as sincere as their father. They listened not to what he said but rather to the way it sounded. It was a dangerous arrangement.

II

The next day, I drove the four hours south to Marshall to visit old friends and get away from the fiancé I couldn't look at. I went to return to the stability of a place I knew and understood, a place that never changed much. Since attending college there, it always provided a sense of comfort, even just thinking about Marshall. As I drove through downtown, I noticed the same three people sitting inside the coffee house, the ones who always came in when I worked there during college. Marshall had a population of 12,000, and its smallness gave me a sense of safety I never had growing up. I looked down at my naked left hand and turned onto Pearle Avenue to Tom's apartment, where I had lived the previous summer.

It felt strange being back after a seven month absence. Tom had asked me to visit several times before, but there was always something more pressing to be done, and I never quite got around to making the trip. The apartment building still smelled like a combination of smoke and cat piss, and most of the light bulbs in the hallway were still in need of replacement. I got to the door and reluctantly knocked, not quite ready to be around people yet even after four hours alone in the car with only my thoughts. Tom opened the door, and I fell into his arms and held his stocky body tight for the first time in half a year. I tugged at his shoulder length dark hair and said, "I missed you like crazy."

I missed you too. Are you hungry?" he asked.

"Yeah, let's go to Perkins."

III

After lunch, I spent the day with Carol, a friend from college, and then drove to Sam's apartment to spend the evening with him and Tom. I had asked Tom over lunch to not get drunk with Sam that evening because Sam was known for his obnoxious and sometimes violent alcohol-induced behavior. I knew it was too much to ask, and when I got to the building and heard them screaming at a movie on television from outside, it was clear that my request had been denied.

"I thought I asked you to not drink tonight," I said as Tom answered the door with a beer in hand.

"Don't you know us at all?" Sam yelled from the other room.

"What are you watching?" I asked.

"Some crazy movie. This guy just lost his hand in battle. It's pretty cool," Sam said.

"Could we maybe turn off the TV and talk?" I asked.

"What for?" Sam asked.

"Because I obviously didn't drive all the way down here to watch a violent movie when I hate watching movies like that in the first place."

"Sam, turn off the TV," Tom said.

"No fucking way," Sam yelled and laughed in the high pitched voice he always used when drunk.

I went into the kitchen, and Tom followed me. "How's it going?" he said and put his sweaty hand on my head.

"I hate this place."

"I know," he said.

"He is such an ass! No wonder he doesn't have a girlfriend. No woman would put up with this," I said and pointed at the wall blanketed with pictures of naked women.

"He had a girlfriend," Tom said.

"Are you talking about Mindy? They never dated. She's suing him for sexual assault," I said and heard an explosion from the other room followed by laughter.

"He didn't do anything. They were both really drunk that night. Cameron was there and told me all about it. Besides, I think she dropped the charges."

"Whatever. I think I want to go home tonight."

"Home to Fargo?"

"Yeah, I shouldn't have come here."

"Why? What's wrong?" he asked and blinked his dark brown eyes at me.

"Carol just spent two hours telling me to stay away from Reed, to not trust him, and here I am thinking about breaking off my engagement for him."

"But is this even really about him?"

25

"Probably not but I would still like to think that the things he said to me were real. She said he's just trying to get me into bed, but why would someone claim to love a girl he's been friends with for years and try to break off her engagement just to get some?"

"If anyone would, we both know it would be Reed," he said, and I had to nod my head. Reed was a guy who would get eight phone numbers in a night, call seven of them, sleep with six of them within a week, and keep the other two girls in his mind for later use. I had seen him have serious relationships too, though, and, from what I could tell, he never made the mistake of cheating.

"What's going on?" Sam said as he stumbled into the kitchen and grabbed the counter top for balance.

"Did Reed talk to you about my situation?" I asked.

"Situation?" Sam said.

"That I might be breaking off my engagement?"

"Yeah, he said something like that, and then he said that you tried to get on him."

"What? He said what? I didn't try to get on him. He's the one who told me that he was in love with me."

"In love with you? What? I never heard anything about that," Sam said and started laughing uncontrollably.

"I can't believe he's doing this. I can't believe I fell for all of it. He must have thought of the whole thing as a joke. I'm never going to talk to him. I'm never going to be anywhere near him again. I can't believe I kissed him," I said and leaned against the refrigerator as tears started forming in my eyes. "I shouldn't be crying about this. I don't cry. I never let people get to me like this," I said and pulled my hair tight to feel something other than anger.

"What's going on?" Sam asked and started to laugh again as he opened the refrigerator and grabbed another beer.

"Tom, I'm going back to your place. You can either give me the keys or come with me. I have to get out of here." He followed me out.

IV

I sat on the floor and looked up at Tom sitting on the old chair with moss green and grey stripes. His shaggy brown hair framed his face, and his breath was filled with the sweet aroma of alcohol. "You have to tell Lynn everything eventually. You know that, right?" he said.

"Everything?" I asked.

"Yeah."

"Even about us?"

"Yeah."

"I know. I've wanted to tell him about last summer since it happened, but every time I was about to I got scared and couldn't bring myself to do it, and now everything with Reed just makes it seem real again, like I'm back here in this apartment with you."

"You are in this apartment with me."

"I know, but it's different now," I said.

"Call him right now."

"What? I can't do that. It's going to kill him if I call him from Marshall to tell him all this," I said and shook my head.

"But you have to. Just do it and get it over with, and I'll be here to help you. Don't keep lying about everything. You can't handle the emotional stress."

"Give me the phone," I said, and he handed me the phone while giving me a slight smile that made my stomach turn as I anticipated the conversation to come.

The phone rang four times, and just as I was about to hang up, Lynn's roommate answered. "Is Lynn there?" I asked, hoping he wasn't.

"Yeah, just a minute."

"Hello," Lynn said.

"Hey, babe."

"Hey. How's Marshall? Are you having a good time with your friends?" he asked.

"Not really. I shouldn't have come. Being here just makes me wish I were back in Fargo again, back with you."

"I'm glad to hear you say that because I miss you, and I was hoping you would be back tomorrow."

"You're not going to be glad I called you, Lynn."

"Why's that?"

"There are a lot of things I need to talk to you about, and part of me wants to wait until I get back to Fargo, but I know I can't do that. I know I have to tell you now."

"Tell me what?"

"Remember last summer when you accused me of cheating on you?"

"What about it?" he asked.

V

Eight months earlier, I spent the summer in Marshall after graduation. There was nothing left for me in that town, but I wasn't ready to see the other side of my life there, so I stayed for three more months to experience the calming intimacy of life in a town I had completely memorized. I lived with Tom because he needed a roommate and because I loved the thrill of deceiving Lynn. During college, Lynn and Tom were conveniently separated by 212 miles of farmland and small towns, but that summer Lynn moved to Marshall and took a job delivering pizzas, so the barrier of distance disappeared.

It was July, and I had just gotten out of the shower. Lynn was supposed to be waiting for me, playing solitaire on the computer, but when I finished I didn't see him sitting at the computer desk. Instead I found a note that read, *Goodbye, Ada. Don't call.* Of course I called.

"Hello," he said.

"Why did you leave? Is this a joke or something?"

"I checked your email, Ada. I know you've been seeing Tom again."

"You what? You invaded my privacy. How could you do that? How did you even know my password?"

"I saw you type it a long time ago, and I told myself I would never use it, but I just had to know. You've been spending less and less time with me, and more time with him again, and I started to get suspicious."

"That is still no reason to invade my privacy like that. I should be the one mad at you."

"Have you been fooling around with your roommate, Ada?"

"No."

"Then why did Brenda say in her email to you that you shouldn't be fooling around with Tom when you're dating me?"

"She was referring to a kiss that we had back in March. You already knew about that."

"She wasn't talking about something going on this summer?"

"No, and you shouldn't have been reading my email anyway. You deserve the pointless worrying when you do things like that."

I sat there on the phone that afternoon as the sun heated up the apartment to unbearable temperatures and lied to him about everything. I found myself smiling more through each lie and feeling a great sense of accomplishment that I could talk my way out of something that would normally be so damning. All I had to do was compose the information in just the right way, and everything was salvaged. I was in control, and Lynn and Tom seemed to enjoy the game too.

VI

I paused for a moment, knowing that my answer could change everything. " Well, I lied to you. I did cheat on you last summer. For the first half of the summer, I was still seeing Tom."

"I can't believe that. You talked me into moving to Marshall to be with you. I worked a shitty job there all summer delivering pizzas and didn't know anyone there but you, and you were still with him the whole time."

"Not the whole time, just the first half of the summer, and then I realized that what I was doing was wrong and horrible for you and for our relationship, and I cut things off. All the stuff between us the last half of the summer was real."

"It's not real anymore," he said. "Not now that I know the truth. God, Ada! You make me sick sometimes."

"I know. Don't hang up. Just listen to me for a minute. We'll work through this. It all happened a long time ago, and it shouldn't change the way things are now. We're going to get married, we're going to be happy, and someday this will all just be a bad memory."

"It's hard to see that now. I'm going to be mad at you for a long time, Ada."

"I know, and I expect that, and I'm okay with that, but you have to promise me that we'll still get married. You have to promise me that we'll work things out."

There was a long pause. "As mad as I am at you right now . . . you know I still love you, and you know that I will eventually forgive you," and just like that I was over the first hurdle, the first major confession of the conversation had been accomplished.

"There is something else I have to tell you," I said.

"Oh no."

"No, it's not as bad as the first thing. I promise."

"What?"

"Reed told me a couple of days ago that he's in love with me."

"I knew you two weren't just friends. You spend way too much time together. You don't even spend that much time . . ."

"Wait. Let me finish explaining. Nothing happened between us, and I thought for a while that he was being sincere, but being in Marshall and talking to people who know him has changed all that. I don't want him. I want you."

"Are you sure because if you change your mind about this when you get back, I don't think I can handle that. I need to know right now that we're going to make things work."

"We are." I said, but I knew it was a lie.

I hung up the phone and looked over at Tom. He had a smirk on his face. "You're beautiful when you lie," he said.

"Why, thank you," I said and threw the cordless phone onto the couch across the room. "Wait a minute," I said. "Did you talk me into calling him for your own entertainment, for a show?"

"I love a good show," he said. Tom was different from other guys I had known. He wasn't interested in the common conventions of life but instead pursued whatever inspired him at the moment. Once, when we were living together, I came home from work early and found him in the livingroom having a philosophical debate with himself. He was flailing his arms and speaking in two distinctly different voices, one with a British accent and one much meeker and more monotone than his own. I stood and watched as he described various hypotheses on the source of morality. After a few minutes, he turned around to see me standing there. I expected him to be mortified from being discovered, but he just waved hello to me, smiled, and went back to his debate. I sat in my room for over an hour listening to the argument unfold, and I realized that he would never bore me.

"Yeah, you always did," I said.

"I wish you still lived here," he said.

"And what would I do? Work at Clifton Coffee for the rest of my life and sleep on your futon?"

"Sounds good to me," he said and kissed me on the forehead.

That night I slept uncomfortably on the couch that was too short for even my five foot frame, waking up constantly and shivering under the one thin blanket I had for warmth. I wanted to get in my car and drive back to Fargo, but something kept me there.

VII

"Did you know it's noon already?" I heard Tom's voice and opened my eyes slightly.

"So?"

"So you should get up and shower so we can have lunch with Sam."

"I really don't know if I'm in the mood after the scene I caused at his place last night. He must think I'm an emotional mess."

"Don't worry. I talked to him an hour ago, and he didn't even remember you were over last night. He was pretty wasted."

"Fine, give me a half hour to get ready," I said.

"Mind if I shower first?"

"It's your place. Go ahead."

While he was in the shower, I started thinking about how I could determine for sure if Reed had been lying to me. I remembered him saying he had told Dave, a professor we had at Prairie State, that he wanted to date me. If I could find out if that were true, I would at least know if his interest for me was genuine, so I pulled out the phonebook and found Dave's number. I told myself that it wasn't completely insane for me to call him since he and I had been friends outside of the classes I took from him, I house-sat for him when he was in Virginia over the summer, and he had Tom and me over for dinner a few times.

"Hi, Dave," I said after he answered. "This is Ada."

"What's going on?"

"I have a question for you, and I normally wouldn't ask you something like this, but I don't know who else to ask."

"Okay . . ."

"Did Reed ever tell you that he wanted to date me?"

"Reed and I don't talk about personal stuff like that, just poetry and the school literary magazine," he said.

"Really? Because Reed said that he told you last year that he was interested in me."

"I suppose it's possible that he may have said something and I just don't remember."

"Did he tell you that I'm thinking about breaking off my engagement?"

"Reed and I haven't talked for months."

"He said he calls you almost every day."

"He did?"

"Yeah, I was under the impression that you two were pretty close."

Dave chuckled a bit and said, "This is really odd."

"Can I ask you something else?" I said, figuring I might as well get all the information I could.

"Shoot."

"Have you ever heard anything about him having a heart problem?"

"Actually, yeah. I did hear something about that. Julie said he told her that last fall."

"Did she say anything specific about it?" I asked.

"Not that I recall, but she's actually going to be over here in about an hour to babysit for Antonia if you want to call back. I'm sure she would be happy to talk to you about all this."

I couldn't believe my luck. "Will you let her know I'm calling?" I asked.

"Yeah, I'll give her the heads up on it."

"Thanks, Dave."

Tom came out of the bathroom with his dark locks dripping down his face and a blue towel wrapped loosely around his waist exposing the top of his pubic hair. "Who were you talking to?"

"Dave."

"Hand me the phone. I'm going to call Sam."

"Can we make it later than we were planning? I have a phone call to make in an hour."

"Yeah, that's fine."

VIII

I felt nervous energy rushing through me before I called Julie, a girl I barely knew well enough to say hi to in a store. We had had a couple of classes together throughout college but never became friends. I forced myself to dial the numbers to Dave's house again, but this time with much more hesitancy.

"Hello," she said, her voice gentle and almost inviting.

"Julie, this is Ada. Did Dave tell you I might call?"

"Yeah, he did. He said you had questions about Reed for me."

"Yeah . . . this is kind of awkward."

"That's okay. Go ahead," she said.

"Okay . . . did you know that I'm engaged?"

"To Reed?" she asked.

"No, no, no, to someone else."

"No, I didn't know that."

"Well anyway, Reed and I had been spending a lot of time together after things with him and Sara didn't work out, and one night he told me that he's wanted to date me for the past three years and that it's killing him that I'm going to marry Lynn."

"Really?"

"Why do you say it like that?" I asked in response to her energized tone.

"You probably don't want to hear this, but after Keith and I broke off our engagement Reed told me the same thing."

"Did he tell you that he had a heart problem too?"

"Yep and that he wasn't supposed to live to see Christmas." She

33

chuckled.

"Are you serious?"

"He told Melanie too. She and I were talking one night, and she brought up the fact that she was thinking about dating Reed. She had never even liked him until he said all that flattering stuff to her, and then when he mentioned the heart problem she decided she should give him a chance."

"Oh, my God! He told Melanie too?"

"I'm glad you called because I wouldn't want anyone to date him. He's a complete psycho," she said.

"Do you think he made up a medical problem as an attempt to get us into bed?"

"I'm sure of it," she said, and we continued to talk as though we had been friends for years, sharing personal details about not only our parallel encounter with Reed but also the messy breakup she went through with her fiancé, Keith, who turned out to be gay, and my current debate on whether or not to marry Lynn.

IX

At Perkins I found myself incapable of eating my eggs and toast and instead moved the food around my plate with a fork. "So Sam, you really don't remember me being at your place last night?"

"I don't remember much of anything from last night," he told me.

"You don't remember telling me that Reed claimed I tried to get on him?"

"I said that?"

"Yeah."

"You should know about that. You were there the night he said that. Remember?" and I suddenly did remember. Reed and I were sitting in his room joking about how we should call Sam and try to convince him that I got really drunk and tried to seduce Reed. We had gotten Sam to believe, on several occasions, that I was drunk, which was proof of Sam's gullible nature since I was afraid of the loss of control alcohol created and never drank more than one glass of anything. This had all happened months before Reed's confession of love for me, and that was what Sam had been referring to. It still didn't change what Julie had said, though.

"I'm going to go take a piss," Sam said.

"I talked to Julie today," I said to Tom after Sam was out of hearing range.

"That's who you were talking to?"

"Yep."

"Well, whatever she said, don't take it too seriously. She's wanted Reed for years, and he's never been very receptive, so she's been known to make up stuff about him."

"According to who? Him?"

"Well, yeah. Look, I think you need to stop listening to everyone else and listen to what you're thinking."

"That's hard to do."

"Just try it for a while."

X

On my drive back to Fargo, I took Tom's advice and kept the radio off in order to focus on my thoughts. With each passing town, I grew more certain of what I needed to do. I decided to break off my engagement to Lynn and to not pursue a relationship with Reed. I decided to try living life by myself for a while and to see where that led me.

I walked into my empty apartment and noticed the blinking red light on my answering machine right away. "Hi, Ada. It's Reed. I hope you had a great time in Marshall with your friends and that you hurry home. I miss you." I put my suitcase in my room and picked up the phone, knowing that talking to him was going to be hard after all the new information I had acquired while in Marshall.

"Hey, Ada," he said, and I remembered that he had caller ID.

"Hey."

"How was your trip?"

"Okay."

"Just okay?"

"I ran into Dave."

"How's he?"

"You should know. You're the one who supposedly talks to him every day."

"It's been a few days."

"Don't you mean a few months? He told me that you two never talk."

"I guess I just told you we did because I wish we did. I really look up to Dave, and I wish we had a better relationship, the kind where you talk every day."

"Reed?"

"Yeah?"

"Are you really dying of a heart problem?"

"I can't believe you doubt me enough to ask me that. Why would I make up something like that?"

"So you really are, and that's the honest answer?"

"Yeah."

"I'm giving you a chance to tell me the truth because I know you're lying about this, and if you tell me the truth now then we can still be friends, and I'll let it go. Why did you tell me you were dying when you're not?"

There was a long pause, and I kept thinking that he was going to hang up, that we would never talk again, and that he would forget about the times when we used to just have fun, the times before he changed everything. "I guess I just wanted there to be a reason when you walked into my apartment and found me there."

"Found you there how? What are you talking about?"

"I've been thinking about suicide a lot lately, and if you found me dead I wanted there to at least be a reason."

"You've seriously been thinking about killing yourself? This isn't another story you're telling?"

"I'm telling you the truth right now. I never talk to anyone about this because it's too embarrassing. People always think I'm strong, but the truth is that I have a lot of hate for myself. I dropped out of college three times, Sara broke up with me, and even my own mother calls me a fuck up."

"Reed, I want to be your friend, but we have to start over with honesty this time and no more lies."

"Okay, I want that too."

"Are you taking anything for the depression?"

"I went to the doctor a couple of weeks ago, and he prescribed medication for me, but I haven't started taking it yet. I think I'm going to start tomorrow."

"Can I see the pills?"

"Sure, come over now, and I'll show them to you." I knew I shouldn't go over there, but he had borrowed a CD of mine, and I at least wanted to get that back.

XI

His apartment had a thick scent of vanilla hanging in the air as it always did, and he answered the door in sweatpants and an old white shirt. "Let me see them," I said while unbuttoning my blue coat. He went to the kitchen briefly before coming back with a small bottle. I looked it over and determined it was authentic, and he handed me a signed note from his doctor on paper from the hospital in Long Creek, his hometown. I decided I believed him about the depression, but it didn't make up for the lies he had told.

"I told you this was real," he said.

"What about your feelings for me? Are they real too?"

"Of course. I wouldn't just make up stuff like that."

"But you made up a heart condition."

"Are you going to hold that against me forever?" he said.

"It was three days ago," I said.

"I already explained that. Trust me. My feelings for you are real. I wouldn't lie about that."

"Did you lie when you told Julie the same thing?"

"Julie?" he said nervously.

"I ran into her this weekend, and she told me that you told her all the same things you said to me."

"I used to have interest in her, but that was a long time ago."

"It was only a couple of months ago."

"A lot can happen in a couple of months."

"And what about Melanie? Did you mean what you said to her?"

"I never said anything like that to Melanie."

"So you're saying she just made it up?"

"If I did say anything to Melanie like that it must've been when I was drunk because I would never normally do that. I don't even find her attractive. You know that."

"You were drunk when you said those things to me," I said.

"Not that drunk. Besides, you know it's different with you," he said.

"I don't know anything with you. You lie so often that I assume everything you say is a lie. I wouldn't even believe that what you said you had for breakfast was true."

"So you're staying with Lynn?"

"I didn't say that, but I can't be with you. I just don't trust you," I said.

"Okay. I understand," he said and walked into the living room, leaving me standing there alone.

I completely forgot about the CD, buttoned up my coat, and left his apartment.

XII

I had asked Lynn to come over so we could talk in person, and every loud engine that I heard zoom by made me jump, thinking it might be him. Finally I heard the knock on the door and shouted, "Come on in."

"I'm really glad you asked me to come over."

"Lynn, we have a lot of serious things to discuss, so you should come and sit by me," I said while patting the blue couch cushion beside me.

"Okay," he said and joined me, instinctively putting his arm around me.

"I love you. You know that, and I always will, but I just don't think our relationship ever recovered after the first time I cheated on you with Tom, and I don't think it ever will. I don't want to plan a wedding with someone who can't trust me, with someone who I haven't even kissed in weeks. We both know something's missing here, something that's needed to make a marriage work, and I think it's time we just admitted that and moved on."

"You're saying you don't want to get married?"

"I'm saying that the past year or so I've started to feel like you're just my friend, and I've been pretending that there's more here than that, but there's not. I can't marry someone who is just a friend, and you deserve more than that too."

"Don't tell me what I deserve. What I deserve is for you to marry me like you promised back in December. What I deserve is for the girl I love to love me back enough to spend her life with me, but I'm obviously not going to get that," he shouted. I looked at Lynn's face. I thought he would cry, but he was filled with rage. My mother said he had a beautiful smile, but I was bored. It was the reason I kissed Tom for the first time and the reason I started spending more time with Reed. Lynn liked to cook together and watch the same movies over and over again, but Reed called me in the middle of the night and convinced me to walk with him on frozen sidewalks until the sun made the city predictable again. Lynn was the path to a conventional life, but Reed was impulsive.

"Lynn, I'm sorry. Do you want me to give you the ring back today or at another time?"

"I don't know how you expect me to think about that right now. I haven't even had time to process what you just said. Are you going to be with Reed now? Is that the real reason for this, that you found someone better?"

"That actually has nothing to do with it. Here," I said and handed him the ring.

"No, keep it for now. I can't handle having this in my apartment," he said and set it on the end table before putting on his shoes and leaving as quickly as he had come.

I loved the idea of him driving across town in a rage, and I knew that he loved it too. The thrill of change and not knowing what existed around the edges of future hours kept us alive. I sat alone and felt the seconds tick into place hesitantly, and I suddenly realized that pain is the same desire as pleasure, the same beautiful reminder that life is real.

XIII

That night the phone rang, and it was Reed. He said he was lonely and that he needed me to come over, that he needed me in general because I was the person who was closest to him, the person who he could most trust. I tried to say no, but somehow I ended up there again.

After that night, we fell back into the friendship we had developed before I went to Marshall, and I managed to forgive the dishonesty we had begun with and even find a sense of amusement in it. The more I focused on the space surrounding me—the postcards of famous poets taped to the walls, the green and orange coffee mugs sitting on end tables, and the notebooks strewn across the floor full of poems that Reed was working on—the more I understood that I could clear away the deception and even enjoy the lie. I could successfully pretend that he did love me, that the things Julie and Dave and anyone else said against him were not important.

Night after night, I found myself drawn back to his apartment, back to the lie. He introduced me to new songs, read aloud from his favorite books of poems, and fed me cheese quesadillas and ice cream. We sometimes stayed up all night as spring snow swirled beyond his bedroom window and trains passed through town and onward to faraway places.

One night, sitting with him on his bedroom floor, he said, "I've always wanted to touch your hair. Is that okay?" I nodded. He rose to his knees, moved toward me, leaned in, and softly ran his fingers through my hair. I was nervous and looking down at the carpet, so he grabbed two handfuls of the hair right above my forehead and pulled my head up. He stared straight at me for a moment and then kissed me. I felt the music and the soft glow of the lamplight and the sweetness of alcohol on his tongue and the warm contrast of his body to the cold outside. I felt all of it rush through me, all at once, and momentarily forgot about the lie. I was in trouble.

I started to sleep beside the lie at night and even found some beauty in it. I learned to admire the talent he had in acting out a story line and even felt honored to have been chosen for the part, and when mornings came, I kissed the lie and found more truth in it than I had known for years.

XIV

In the weeks that followed, the problem arose that I had started to forget the foundation on which the relationship between Reed and I had been built. I had started to love him beyond the pleasure of deception, to forget that the lie even existed and that new lies were being created all the time with each word he spoke.

We sat on his bed one Tuesday afternoon after getting chocolate malts from the Tastee Freez, and he said, "Are you really planning to transfer to Florida next year?"

"Yeah, that's the plan right now. Are you going to miss me?"

He looked at me intensely until I looked up at him, and he said, "Wherever you are that's where I'll be. I want to come with you next year. I mean that. I love you, and I don't ever want to not be with you."

"Are you serious? You would really move across the country to be with me?" I asked.

"I'm dead honest. I wouldn't lie about something like this. That's such a shitty thing to do," he said, and I felt myself slipping away from the game I intended our relationship to be and into something dangerous.

XV

With each passing day the intensity rose, and the lies disguised themselves better and better until I couldn't even label them anymore. We played our roles perfectly. He sent me cards with poems written on the inside, and I called him every day after work or class. We spent our nights in the dim lighting of his room exploring each other, and I fell asleep beside him after long conversations about music and poetry. He started saying things like, "I want to be with you and only you, always only you," and "Ada, I want to spend my whole life with you. I want you to be my wife." The rest of my life fell away from me, and the only thing that mattered was that room. I found myself counting away hours at work and school, wishing for a quick passage of time that would bring me back to him.

I even started to tell my friends that I was going to marry Reed. The

41

ones who had never met him were excited that I seemed so happy, but those who knew Reed were worried.

XVI

Reed spent two weeks in Oklahoma with his grandma visiting his uncle. During that time I listened to music that reminded me of him and spent each day waiting for its end so that I would be one day closer to his return. It was behavior I hadn't exhibited since high school, and I felt ashamed but couldn't get myself to stop.

Carol called me the day Reed flew into Minneapolis and said, "Ada, I don't know how to tell you this, but I'm your friend, so I think I have to."

"Tell me what?" I said and felt my heart beat get faster. "Is this about Reed?" I asked.

"Ada, he's been telling his friends that you two are just friends, that you've never been anything more."

"Are you serious?"

"I'm sorry, but I had to tell you."

"Who did he say that to?"

"Well, I heard from Cindy that I work with that her husband, Chris, who is friends with Reed heard from some guys at school . . ."

"What guys?"

"Well, Cindy didn't remember their names."

"So you're telling me that you heard this fourth-hand and that you don't even know who the people are that Reed supposedly said this to?"

"You know he can't be trusted, Ada. Why are you giving him the benefit of the doubt?"

"Because being with him is an adventure, and I told myself from the beginning of this that I knew it would end and that it would be hard for me when it did but that I had to do this anyway."

"Why would you put yourself in this situation when you know you're going to get hurt?"

"Because I have to. Look—I spent three years with Lynn, and everything was so predictable."

"Lynn is a great guy. He's the right kind of guy, the guy you should want to marry."

"I know. Do you think I don't know that? I just wasn't ready yet. I started to feel trapped . . . like I was suffocating."

"I know, but I can see where this is heading with Reed, and it's not good," she said.

"I know, but I'm being careful. Don't worry. I'm gonna get going, okay? I have a paper due tomorrow."

"Okay. Try to have a good night," she said, and I hung up the phone.

Less than five minutes passed before the phone rang again, and it was Reed. "I'll be home tomorrow," he said.

"Can we talk?"

"Can it wait until I get back tomorrow?"

"I would prefer to talk now," I said.

"I was just on my way out the door to drive my grandma home."

"Will you call me when you get to her place?"

"How about if I call you tomorrow?"

"It's really important that I talk to you tonight. Don't worry; it's not bad. It's a good thing," I lied.

"It is?"

"Yeah."

"Okay, I'll call you in a half hour."

XVII

I picked up the phone on the second ring and, after confirming it was him, said, "Why have you been telling your friends that we're just friends and nothing more and then telling me that you love me and want to marry me?"

"Whoa, slow down. I haven't been telling people that we're just friends. Where did you get that idea?"

"Carol heard that you said that," I said.

"Be more specific," he said and sighed loudly into the phone.

"Carol called me and told me tonight that she had heard from Cindy, who heard from Chris, who heard from some guys at school that you had been saying that." I realized how ludicrous it sounded right after it came out of my mouth.

"And you know the Marshall rumor-mill is always one hundred percent accurate," he said in a sarcastic tone.

"I'm not saying that I don't believe you. It's just hard when one of my best friends calls me just to tell me about this."

"It's up to you whether or not you want to believe me, but you don't have much reason not to based on the information Carol gave you."

"It also made me mad that you didn't want to call me back tonight. I should at least be important enough to you to want to talk to me when we haven't seen each other for two weeks," I said.

"You said the four words."

"Four words?" I asked.

"Yeah, 'we need to talk.'"

"So?"

"So those words usually don't mean something positive. I thought that maybe you and Lynn were getting back together, considering I was gone for two weeks."

"No. Lynn and I are not getting back together," I said, and I could hear Reed sigh into the phone again, but it didn't sound like a sigh of relief.

XVIII

There were times when even he seemed to forget about the presence of the lie. We were sitting in Mom's Kitchen eating dinner one night when he looked at me and said, "Are we okay?"

"What do you mean?"

"It seems like you haven't been as affectionate toward me lately, and you've been spending several nights a week with Lynn."

"Lynn and I are still friends, and if I've been less affectionate, I'm sorry. It wasn't something I was consciously doing. Does it bother you that Lynn and I hang out so much?"

"Kind of," he said and looked down at his cheeseburger.

"Why?"

"It makes me worry that you two are rekindling something," he said while still looking at his plate instead of me.

"I won't spend so much time with him if it bothers you. You never said anything before."

"Do you really love me, or am I just someone to fill the void?" he asked.

"You know I love you. I'm the one who should be worrying about whether or not you love me. When I tell you that I want to spend the rest of my life with you, I'm being honest. I really do want you to move to Florida with me, not just because you're someone but because you're you. I think you are one of the most amazing people," and then I looked at him and noticed tears streaming down his face as he wiped them away with his sweatshirt sleeve and looked everywhere but at me. "Are you crying?"

"I'm not used to being emotional like this," he said.

"What's wrong?" I asked and looked around the restaurant to see if anyone was watching.

"Nothing's wrong. I just love you so much, and you make me feel things that other people can't," he said, and we sat there in silence while I tried to dissect the weeks of deception and pleasure that had led up to the moment of his breakdown. I looked at his eyes and found nothing but sincerity behind them, and I lost the ability to remind myself that being able to cry on demand is a trick every actor must master.

XIX

"I've thought a lot about this, and I can't keep the ring, Lynn," I said to him while driving home from Happy Hugo's Pizza and Ice Cream.

"I want you to have it," he said while looking out the window at the passing landscape of old houses.

"I just wouldn't feel right about having it. Besides, what would I do with it?"

"Just put it in a box somewhere and take it out from time to time and think of me."

"You know we're not getting married, right?" I said.

"I know," he said.

"So I wouldn't feel comfortable having something worth three thousand dollars just sitting in a box, and I have a lot of other beautiful things you've given me to remind me of you."

"Well, I wouldn't feel right knowing that someone else is wearing the ring that I bought for you. Please keep it, and just promise me you won't ever pawn it."

"I would never do that," I said.

"Good," he said, and I wondered how much the ring would go for.

XX

There were issues with Reed that went beyond the collection of lies that should have kept me away. One problem was the fact that he was twenty-seven and still living completely off of his parents' money. He hadn't had a job the entire time he lived in Fargo, which was four months, and he hadn't had a job for over a year before that either. The last semester of his senior year in college he just stopped going to classes. His excuse was that when his great-grandma died he couldn't handle the emotional stress of the situation and so he certainly could not deal with the stresses that school brought.

Somehow, though, I managed to look past the fact that he had no ambition or even self-respect, and I even found it somewhat cute that he didn't work and spent all his time going to coffee shops, writing poems on napkins, and making home videos by standing in front of the television with his video camera and taping his favorite scenes from movies. The complete lack of responsibility in his life had contrasted with my world so much that I enjoyed living vicariously through him.

XXI

I went home to St. Paul for the weekend after spending a week of evenings with Reed bowling, going out to dinner, playing cards at his apartment, going to the movies, and taking long walks. Reed headed to Minneapolis to spend the weekend at his brother's apartment. He and I had agreed that he would come over Sunday evening for an hour or two to meet my parents. He said he wanted to meet them before we got engaged, but he called an hour after he was supposed to show up, saying that his car had been shaking when he drove under forty miles per hour and that he was afraid to drive all the way across the Twin Cities with his car acting up.

"How are you going to drive home tomorrow then?" I asked.

"If it does it tomorrow at least car repair shops will be open, but today is Sunday, so if my car stalls I'm screwed," he said.

"When is the last time you drove it?"

"Yesterday."

"Will you at least go out and drive a bit now to see if it's still doing that?"

"I'll do that for you," he said, but I knew he would just sit around for ten minutes before calling me back to say that the car was still driving poorly.

He called back and said just that, followed by, "You should come over here."

"To your brother's place?"

"Yeah. Why not? It would be fun, and you could meet him, his roommates, and his girlfriend."

"I think I should just stay here. I'll see you back in Fargo."

"But I really want to see you tonight," he said.

We talked about it for over an hour, and eventually he talked me into driving to uptown Minneapolis to stay overnight at his brother's place before heading home the next day. My parents saw me frantically packing my suitcase, and my dad said, "Why are you packing now? Aren't you leaving in the morning?"

"Change of plans. I'm actually going to Minneapolis to Reed's brother's place."

"I thought Reed was coming over here," my mom said.

"His car isn't working so well, and he's scared to drive it across the Cities tonight, so I'm going over there."

"And you're going to spend the night there?" my dad asked.

"That's the plan."

"How many beds do they have there? Where are you going to sleep? Do you need to bring a sleeping bag or sheets or anything?" my mom asked.

"Nope."

"Where are you going to sleep?" my dad asked.

"I'm twenty-three. Please don't treat me like I'm fifteen," I said.

"Are you having sex with him?" my mom asked.

"Mom, just because we sleep in the same bed does not mean we're having sex. Lynn and I slept in the same bed every night and never had sex."

"You and Lynn slept in the same bed every night? You have your own apartment. Why would you be sleeping at his place every night?" she asked.

"We didn't sleep at his place every night. He stayed at my apartment too." I wished I could take those words back as I imagined my parents picturing my single bed.

"I don't think it's appropriate for you to sleep with him at his brother's. What is his brother going to think?" asked my mom.

"Considering that his brother sleeps with his girlfriend every night, he probably won't think anything of it," I said.

"We really wanted to talk to you about Florida tonight, but now that you're leaving we won't have a chance."

"What about Florida?" I asked.

"We're just worried about how this is all going to work. Have you actually sat down and written out a budget for next year? I know you think they're paying you a lot to be a research assistant, but it's not that much when you break it down month to month, and we're not going to pay for your car insurance anymore, so I don't know how you're going to afford having a car, and if you don't have a car down there how will you get around? How are you planning to get to Florida in the first place? We might be able to bring you down there with the van full of your stuff, but we haven't even discussed this yet . . ." As I listened to her drone on and on about reasons my plans wouldn't work, I tuned it out until she said, "You always involve us so much in your plans and then expect us to drop everything and help you . . ."

"I don't need your help. Look, Reed is planning to move to Florida with me. He said I could share his car with him, and we're going to rent a U Haul, so I don't need you guys to help me move, so can we please just drop it?"

"He's what? Are you two going to live together?" my mom asked.

"No. We're not going to live together, but we're probably going to get engaged this summer. I don't expect you to be happy about this . . ."

"Good. You got it!" my dad blurted out, and I left them sitting there and went back to my room to finish packing.

XXII

The drive to Minneapolis went smoother than I anticipated, and I didn't get lost until I was within a block of his brother's house, and even then I quickly found my way back to the streets from the directions Reed gave me.

I knocked on the door, and a guy I recognized from pictures opened it. "You must be Nate," I said to the blond standing in the doorway.

"Yep."

"I'm Ada," I said and held out my hand.

He shook it and said, "Reed's in the shower." He pointed to the bathroom down the hall and disappeared into one of the bedrooms. I stood in the hallway alone and listened to the mixture of Nate and his girlfriend talking and the loud fan coming from the bathroom.

After about ten minutes, Reed opened the bathroom door, towel drying his hair and smiling invitingly at me. "You made it," he said. I wanted to be upset that he made me drive thirty miles across the city and wasn't ready when I got there, but as soon as I saw him I was transfixed by the smell of men's body wash and the way his voice echoed off the wooden floors in the narrow hallway.

We spent the evening in an empty room upstairs playing cards and table tennis. His brother's house was the kind of house I had dreamed about as a kid. The downstairs had all the essentials of living, but the upstairs was a wonderland of games and colorful furniture. Old arcade games lined one of the walls, the pool table and ping pong table sat in the center of the room, and a bookshelf filled with board games and movies stood in the corner. Nate was just like Reed, a thirty-six-year-old law school student who didn't seem very motivated to graduate and spent his free time learning exotic recipes and taking international trips.

"You should come to Long Creek with me tomorrow and then to Marshall with me to have dinner with my grandma," Reed said after we finished our last game of table tennis.

"I can't. I have class tomorrow night."

"Skip it."

"You know I can't do that. I never skip class. I only miss classes if I'm actually sick."

"Which is all the more reason to do it just once to see what it feels like."

"What about your car? I thought you were going to stick around and get it fixed," I said.

"Nah, it'll be fine. It only does that for city driving, and, other than the first few miles, it's highway driving all the way."

"What are we going to do in Long Creek?" I asked. "I don't think I'm ready to meet your parents yet."

"You don't have to meet them. They're in Toronto this week visiting my brother, Joel. Remember?"

"So why even go there?"

"I want to shower at my house, and it's on the way to Marshall. We could eat lunch at the Dari King," he said, and for some reason that small detail almost sold me on the idea. I had always driven past the outdoor ice cream shack on the way to Marshall from my house while I was a college student, but I never thought much of it. The way Reed said it made this obscure place seem important.

"So you expect me to drive all the way to Marshall and then back up to Fargo in one day?"

"No, you can spend the night with me in Marshall and leave for Fargo on Tuesday." After an hour of discussion, I finally said, "Okay, I'll come."

That night we fell asleep on a cot next to the window in the upstairs of the old Minneapolis house. I listened for the sound of mice scurrying across the wooden floor but only heard the steady ticking of an old clock.

XXIII

I watched Reed's car through my rear-view mirror more than I watched the road as I drove the two and a half hours from Minneapolis to Long Creek. I felt guilt, knowing I should have been driving to Fargo for class and asked myself why I had agreed to his plan in the first place, but it was always like that with Reed. I was constantly finding myself in situations that went against my better judgment. I knew the invitation to come with him was only a test to see what he could get me to do, and I was disappointed in myself for failing.

When I got to Long Creek, a small town on the prairie with a population of 4,900, I pulled into the Dari King, and Reed's car followed.

"I can't believe you talked me into this," I said as he stepped out of his car.

"Eating at Dari King?"

"No, just this whole thing. The whole time I was driving here I kept thinking about how crazy this is. I should just drive up to Fargo right now. I could still get there in plenty of time for class."

"Come on, you came this far. Besides, I want you to meet my grandma."

XXIV

Dinner at his grandma's consisted of a frozen pizza and cans of coke, and after we ate, Reed and I moved all the furniture from her living room to the garage so the carpets could be cleaned the following day. It was clear that she didn't know we were coming, and I couldn't believe I had driven all that way just to move furniture and eat pizza. I kept thinking about the class I was missing in Fargo.

"I'm going to go over to Josh's for a while," I said outside of his grandma's house. "Where can I reach you later?"

"I'll be at Patrick's," he said and pulled out a piece of paper and a pen to write down the number.

XXV

I stood outside of Josh's dorm room, hoping he would be home.

I knocked, and he yelled, "Who is it?"

"Ada."

He opened the door wearing only a white towel and shouted, "What the hell are you doing in Marshall?"

"I came with Reed."

"Don't you have class?"

"He talked me into it."

"Interesting . . . Damn, girl! It's so good to see you again."

I sat on the bed and watched out of the corner of my eye while Josh changed into sweatpants and a hooded sweatshirt.

"So you're still with Reed?" he asked. "I'm telling you, girl, he's not good enough for you."

"Who is?"

"You're looking at him," he said.

"I'm pretty sure if we were going to date we would have done it during the two years that we lived in the same zip code," I said.

"Don't think I didn't try," he said.

"Sorry. It's the brother-sister syndrome. There's nothing I can do."

"I'm too black to be your brother."

"Damn, that's right. You're black."

"It looks like you need a new excuse."

"I guess so," I said.

"Well, as long as the guy makes you happy then I'm happy for you," he said.

"Happy is definitely not the word for it. It's crazy, Josh. I know he's lying to me all the time about everything, but I just have to go along for the ride to see where this leads. It's so much more interesting than Lynn."

"Trust me. I remember. This is exactly what you said before you started messing around with Tom. Just be careful."

"I don't want to be careful," I said.

"Okay. Well, just know that I'll be here if things don't work out," he said.

"I might just take you up on that."

XXVI

When I got to Patrick's trailer, I knocked repeatedly. No one bothered to answer, so I just walked in. I started to take my shoes off but realized the floor was dirtier than my tennis shoes, so I kept them on. Patrick walked into the kitchen to grab a beer, saw me, and yelled, "Hey, Reed. Your chick's here."

"Send her in," I heard him yell, so I left the tiny kitchen and entered the living room. Reed was sitting on the couch with a couple of guys I knew from college. They were drinking beer, smoking pot, and laughing about nothing.

Patrick appeared, balancing several beer cans in his arms, and said, "Theo, have another beer."

He threw it to the huge guy sitting in the corner. "I don't think I should," Theo said. He had had gastric bypass surgery a few months before and wasn't supposed to be drinking because his stomach couldn't handle the alcohol.

"Come on, just one more. You look like you need it," Patrick said, and Theo grabbed the can and started to drink. I couldn't believe guys who were almost thirty could still be so susceptible to peer-pressure.

The air in the trailer was a mixture of pot, dirty dogs, and sweat. The three scraggly dogs ran back and forth through the living room and kitchen as Reed's friends sunk into the furniture and continued to laugh about nothing. I sat on the floor and wished I had gone to class instead.

XXVII

Theo and the other guy left, and Patrick went to bed, leaving Reed and me alone. "I'm going to sleep on the recliner," I said. "I have a blanket in my car. I'll go and get it."

"Patrick gave us a blanket," he said, "and you're not sleeping on the recliner. You should sleep on the couch with me."

"Do you have any idea how uncomfortable that is going to be? We can't both fit on that little couch."

"Sure we can," he said and patted the two inches of remaining couch space I was supposed to somehow sleep on.

"This is never going to work," I said.

"It will be fine," he said. "Lay here with me and enjoy the glow of the moonlight." I lay down beside him, not quite able to fit my whole body on the couch, but the moon shining in through the few bent mini-blinds almost made me forget how dirty the room was and how uncomfortable I was going to be until morning. "What would you say if I asked you to marry me right now?" he asked.

"I would say yes," I said and stared at the brown dog sleeping in the corner.

"Will you marry me?" he said and placed his hand on my face to pull it toward his.

"You can't do that. If you're going to ask me it has to be real. You have to have a ring and everything," I said.

"I know, but I'm asking you in a hypothetical way," he said. I closed my eyes for a moment and thought about the night Lynn asked me to marry him. There was nothing hypothetical about the room filled with candles and rose pedals or the way his eyes looked as he kneeled before me and asked me the question that two years had led up to.

"So ask me again," I said, knowing that the hypothetical would be all I would ever get from Reed.

"Ada Hendricks, will you marry me?" he asked and kissed my cheek.

"Yes, I'll marry you," I said, "but I'm sleeping on the recliner."

"No," he said and pulled me back down to him.

I stayed there all night watching him sleep comfortably as I tried to just remain on the couch. With each passing hour he sprawled out more, and I clung harder to the side, waiting for morning to come. I studied his face, and even the small wrinkles around his eyes and thin chapped lips were beautiful to me; his imperfections were more attractive than the best features on the other faces I had seen. I watched the first light of morning wake the dark corners of that room and wished I could at least know what he was dreaming.

XXVIII

Reed and I stood in the hallway at Prairie College that second afternoon in Marshall and talked to his friend, Nadine. "So are you going to walk in the graduation ceremony in May?" she asked him.

He looked at her and then at me before saying, "I think so."

"What are you talking about?" I said, shooting him a perplexed look. "You never graduated."

"What? You never graduated?" Nadine said to him.

He looked at his sandals and said, "Technically no."

This wasn't the first school related lie I had ruined for him. When his friends came to Fargo one weekend to visit, I heard them ask him how the semester was going. I informed them that he wasn't taking classes in Fargo, and he acted like he had told them and they just forgot. I wondered how a person could base his whole life on falsehoods and whether or not he started to believe the lies he told so often and so easily. I loved watching his interactions with others and with me, treating each statement he made as a puzzle and trying to work with the given information to get at something true. The problem was that I often discovered that the given was false as well, and I would have to start back at the beginning again.

XXIX

I left Marshall that day without his white car following me. He asked me to stay and spend the night with him at his parents' cabin, but I had school and work calling me back up north. I assumed he would be back sometime the following day, but the next day came and went, and I didn't hear from him. Two more days passed before I received a short email saying that he didn't want to get in the way of my studying, so he was going to stay at the cabin a while longer. The next week, I only got two more emails, each one shorter than the one before and still no mention of when he might return.

I remembered hearing him say once, while we were still only friends, that he had dated a girl in Fairmont for two months and just moved out of town one day without even letting her know. I laughed at the time, not knowing that someday it would be me. I pictured him loading his couches, dishes, books, clothes, and the bed we had slept on into a U Haul and leaving his Fargo apartment without so much as a second glance.

He sent one more email a few weeks later that said, *You are all I think about when I cannot sleep and all I dream about when I can.*

I never heard from him again.

Prairie Lake's Fall Play

I saw the flier in the drugstore window downtown, and the bright yellow color forced me to read it:

> Prairie Lake proudly announces a fall performance of Beauty and the Beast! Auditions—May 1, 2, and 3 from 7-9 p.m. at Lincoln Middle School.

My eyes scanned the paper quickly, and I walked inside to buy toothpaste, soap, envelopes, cream of potato soup, and a birthday card for my aunt. I didn't think about the flier while inside, but after I paid for my items and passed through the glass doors, I again found myself drawn to that yellow paper. Suddenly I imagined myself in Belle's yellow dress, floating across a stage, singing to an audience of people I saw every day.

I was a travel agent, and, eight years into my career, the tedious routine of planning exotic getaways, romantic adventures, historic tours, and fun family trips started to take its toll. The travel industry was folding in on itself quickly as most people could plan their own trips on the internet. We eventually catered to the rich and elderly, and our one office served three counties. My salary was no longer what the informational brochure at my college had advertised for travel agents, and I had to agree to a cut in pay twice just to keep my position at Southern Star Tours. I could no longer afford even a weekend trip to Sioux Falls, so my life was limited to the office and evenings in front of the TV.

I started thinking that maybe participating in the town play was just what I needed. I could meet someone new, experience the thrill of late nights memorizing lines and dance moves, and maybe even learn undiscovered things about myself.

At work the next day, I kept thinking about what it would feel like to audition. What would I sing? What would I wear?

During lunch hour, an overweight man wearing tight khaki pants and a white button-down shirt came into the office. "Mind if I put my sign in your window? We're putting on a community production of Beauty and the Beast, and I need to advertise the auditions."

"Sure, go ahead," I said and smiled. I wanted to ask him questions about how the audition process worked (the only knowledge I had was from the movies), but instead I turned back to my work as he quickly taped the paper to the window and exited the office.

It was hard to concentrate on Mary and Phillip Dunn's trip to the Everglades. I kept noticing the sign, and I wondered who would play The Beast.

I never planned on being single at thirty-two, but Prairie Lake, a town with a population of nine-thousand, was the only place I got a job offer after college, and most of the men in town were either married or just killing time and right out of high school. I had heard that sometimes the local community college hired men to teach, but I didn't know how to meet them. Since they had summers off, maybe they would participate in a town production, I thought.

As I scribbled down notes on Southern Florida restaurants and hotel options, my life in Prairie Lake seemed to open up again. I suddenly had that feeling of possibilities, the same feeling I had the first few months I lived there, back when I was fresh from college and ready for the world. I looked out the window and noticed the pink buds forming on the tree across the street, and I wrote down the audition dates in my desk calendar.

* * *

During the two weeks leading up to the audition, I watched my copy of *Beauty and the Beast* several times. I had long brown hair and a decent figure for my age, so it seemed likely that I would get the part.

Before I knew it, I was there, standing in the back of the auditorium at Lincoln Middle School. The overweight man I had met that afternoon at the travel agency was sitting at a table with a clipboard in his hands, and a middle-aged woman with short curly hair sat beside him. There was no one else in the room.

He spotted me and yelled, "Come on up. Get on the stage, and show us what you got."

I walked down the aisle, ascended the stairs to the stage, set my purse down, and looked at the two judges seated at the table on the side of the stage. It wasn't what I had imagined. It was nothing like the reality TV shows that seek to find a musical star. They were supposed to be below me, looking up at the stage, and the auditorium was supposed to be filled with onlookers, nervous for their turn but still cheering me on. Somehow the absence of the ritual made me more nervous. I hadn't prepared for such an intimate affair, and I felt like I was in high school again, expecting to kiss a boy while he was expecting much more.

"What are you going to sing for us?"

"A Change in Me," I said.

"Okay, go ahead," he said.

I got through the song without any problems—no voice cracks, forgotten lyrics, or noticeable shakiness in my held notes. I was feeling pretty good about my performance.

"We'll let you know," he said, and I left the room with a smile on my face.

* * *

A few days later I got home from work and noticed a blinking light on my answering machine. I pressed play. "Hi, Jessica." It was him! "I wanted to let you know that we completed auditions and decided on the parts. We really liked your audition and would like to offer you the part of The Menu." I stood there stunned. I pressed play again, but he said the same thing—The Menu. *The Menu?* I searched my memory for an image. I had watched the movie repeatedly in the days leading up to that message and didn't remember seeing The Menu character. I had played out the cast of characters in my mind, and I was fine with being Mrs. Potts, The Featherduster, or even The Wardrobe, but The Menu was totally unacceptable. I decided not to accept the role.

* * *

That decision stuck for exactly nineteen hours until my lunch break the next day. Mr. Stark, the director, walked into the travel agency. "Just popping by to take down my sign out front and to make sure you got my message last night."

"Yep, I got it," I said.

"Good, good. We're excited to get going on this. Rehearsals start next Tuesday at six," he said.

"Sounds good," I said. Maybe it would be a good thing, I thought. Just because I was playing a "nobody" character, it didn't mean I couldn't get something out of the experience. I could still meet people. I could be the best damn Menu that play had ever seen.

* * *

I showed up for the first rehearsal the following Tuesday night and noticed him immediately. A burly yet handsome thirtyish man wearing a flannel shirt and corduroy pants stood on the side of the stage. I had never seen him before, but I liked the way he was standing, kind of leaning against nothing as though he was propped up by air. I walked right over to him. Hell, if I was going to do the stupid play to be social, I might as well start out right. "Hi," I said.

"Hey, what's up?"

"I'm Jessica, otherwise known as The Menu."

"Impressive! I'm Carl, otherwise known as The Beast," he said and shook my hand.

"Dang! I would have felt so much better about this exchange if you had a lame role too," I said.

"Hey, there's nothing lame about The Menu. How would the other characters order if you weren't here?"

"So true. Speaking of ordering, I came here straight from work and haven't eaten dinner yet. Do you want to grab a bite after this is done?" I couldn't believe myself. I was acting already. I may have been shy in normal life, but as The Menu I was bold.

"Sure. Let's go to Ruby's," he said.

For the next two hours, I endured hoards of obnoxious children. I hadn't realized when I signed up to do the play that the majority of the actors would be children and high school kids. In my mind, it would be a lot like Broadway, just not as polished. I would later learn that a lot of parents used the community theater as a free babysitting service. There were kids as young as seven in the chorus, and more than half of the rehearsal time was consumed with Mr. Stark and his assistant trying to discipline the unruly kids. We learned "Be Our Guest," and the unimportant roles, like mine, sat around for most of the rehearsal while the main characters practiced their scenes. Still, it was better than watching the same reruns of *The Cosby Show* or sitting through another episode of an *E! True Hollywood Story*.

When rehearsal was over, I met Carl outside. He was leaning against his old truck, and he looked much sexier than the cartoon version of the prince who used to be The Beast. The cartoon prince was too pretty, too feminine, an exact opposite of his Beast counter-part. Carl was the optimal mixture of man and Beast. He had a nicely trimmed beard, a solid body, and a tall stature, but he had bright blue eyes, soft looking hands, and full crimson colored lips.

"Jump in. I'll drive," he said, and I happily followed his orders. I didn't know if it was a date or not, but it felt like one. He was driving, I was nervous, and we were going to have dinner. I couldn't believe my luck.

We were seated at a table near the bar. "You're going to have to be pretty entertaining if you want to keep my attention. The weather channel is on," he said and nodded at the TV behind me.

"I'll see what I can do," I said and smiled.

"How long have you lived in Prairie Lake?" he asked, and I was relieved that he led us off with a boring question. It took some of the pressure off me.

"It's been about eight years," I said.

"Wow. How old are you?" he asked, and I was suddenly embarrassed about my age. It hadn't occurred to me that Carl might be a lot younger than me. I just assumed he was around thirty, but I realized the beard may have added years to his appearance.

I thought about lying but said, "Thirty-two."

"Not bad," he said.

"How old are you?"

"Twenty-four," he said, and the restaurant suddenly felt a lot colder. I looked up and realized I was sitting directly under an air vent.

"I'm sorry. I thought you were older. I think it's the beard or maybe the low voice."

"That's true. Voices don't usually change until around thirty," he said and smiled.

"Anyway, it doesn't really matter. It's not like we're on a date. We're just hanging out and hopefully venting about how annoying those kids were tonight."

"This isn't a date?" he asked and scratched his chin.

"I don't think so."

"Damn! I was assuming it was."

"Did you want it to be?" I asked and held my breath.

"Of course." The room seemed to heat up again, and I sat back in my chair.

"Well, alright then."

"Unless I'm too young for you . . ."

"I think I can handle it," I said. "How long have you lived here?"

"Just a few months. I lived up in Fargo for a while, but I didn't like being that close to Canada."

I didn't know if he was joking or not, so I laughed and said, "Who would?"

"Yeah, plus I went to school for teaching but discovered, after a year of it, that I don't like kids."

"After tonight's display, I can see why," I said. "So what are you doing now?"

"Not sure yet. My parents live here, so I'm making myself at home in their basement until I figure it all out. I figure it doesn't become pathetic until the age of thirty . . . no offense."

"None taken. I don't live with my parents," I said and surveyed the room for familiar faces.

"You have a pretty figure. I noticed it while you were learning the dance steps for 'Be Our Guest.' Not too curvy . . . very girlish. I like that."

"Are you saying I have the body of a middle school kid?"

"Yeah, but in a really cute way."

"Thanks. You're pretty cute too." I hadn't been on a date in years, and it was all going so well. I told him things I wouldn't normally say on a first date—like the fact that I daydreamed of being Belle and was secretly crushed when I was offered the part of The Menu. He laughed and made me feel comfortable, so I told him other things—like the intense fear of flying I developed after September 11th, the fact that all vegetables tasted the same to me, my inability to tear up during happy moments, and my habit of chewing on the skin around my fingernails.

We stayed at Ruby's for three hours before he drove me back to my car. The middle school parking lot was deserted when we rolled in around midnight. He pulled up to my car, and I said, "Are you going to kiss me?"

"I don't think you're supposed to ask. It ruins the scene."

"We're in a play together, so I figured our real life interaction could be less theatrical."

"I don't think The Beast and The Menu interact much in the play," he said.

"Just answer the question," I said, and he leaned over to me, grabbed the back of my neck, and pulled my mouth into his. I had never kissed a bearded man before, and I had to stay focused to remain on target. Any wrong move brought me away from the lips and over to the treacherous territory of fur, but, for a moment, I felt like Belle kissing The Beast, and I enjoyed being the star of the show.

* * *

As the play progressed, it was getting harder and harder to focus at work. I caught myself daydreaming about Carl when I should have been working on Joyce Kephart's trip to Spain or Jerry Mislow's West Texas road-trip. Being in the community play had somehow become just what I'd imagined (minus the part about me being the star of the show). I was not only learning how to act on stage but in my life as well. At thirty-two I had only had a handful of boyfriends, and those relationships never really went anywhere. There was Tony, the guy I met online who never wanted to introduce me to his friends; Seth, the paranoid pot-head who only dated me for three weeks and probably just to have someone "normal" to introduce to his parents when they visited from out of state; Ken, the one who turned out to be gay; and Steve, the guy who only called me after midnight and always wanted to get drunk and have sex. Carl seemed different, though. Even my previously skeptical friends started to become optimistic when I explained to them that Carl took me on dates, often paid for my meals, and sometimes left sweet notes on my car for me to find when I got off work.

Carl took me to Sioux Falls for the day one Saturday for shopping and the opportunity to eat at a new restaurant. We had time to kill before dinner, so he suggested going down to the falls. "I've actually never been there. Can you believe that? I've lived here all this time, been to Sioux Falls dozens of times, and I've never seen the falls," I said.

"I had a feeling," he said. "That's why we need to go. You're gonna love it."

We had been dating a little over a month; we were right at the point where my relationships usually started going south, but I couldn't see any such signs in my relationship with Carl. "How many times have you been here?" I asked.

"I take all my girlfriends here," he said and winked at me. It was the first time he called me his girlfriend, and I could start to see the future path that spread out before us. My mother always said to not get ahead of myself, but this was just all too perfect— I had envisioned meeting him, and now I was in his car for a Saturday road-trip to a place I'd never been.

"Well then it's a good thing we're going," I said.

He parked the car in the lot at Falls Park, and we made our way down the concrete path. There weren't many people at the park that day. It was unseasonably hot, so maybe the locals opted for a day inside at the mall instead. We found a bench near the falls, and he said, "Isn't this great?"

The truth is that the scenery alone wasn't really that great. As a travel agent, I had planned trips to Niagara Falls, Victoria Falls, and Yosemite. Of course I was planning those trips for other people and didn't personally visit the places, but after hours of pouring over pictures on informational websites, I had a certain expectation of what a proper waterfall should look like. This was not it. The water at Falls Park was not violent and dangerous, and it didn't plunge to the earth from great heights. Instead it meandered down the rocks and settled in a calm pool at the bottom of the incline. "Yeah, it is," I said and kissed him.

"I think this could really be something."

"The falls?"

"No. Us," he said.

"Yeah, I was thinking that too," I said and snuggled up next to him on the green park bench.

* * *

The next week in practice things were finally starting to come together. The main actors knew their lines, and I could finally sing the alto part on the songs where the women were split into two sections. My only real concern was whether or not I would have the grace and stamina to perform the choreography while sandwiched between the two large pieces of cardboard that made up my costume. Mr. Stark assured me that there would be plenty of time to adjust to the costume during the two days of dress rehearsal. Besides, I was in the back for most of the songs, so it didn't really matter if I missed a step or two anyway.

We were right in the middle of practicing "The Mob Song" when it happened. Pam Hanson, a middle-aged woman and mother of three children in the play, rushed into the auditorium. "Stop!" she screamed, and Sadie, her beautiful daughter who had the privilege of playing Belle, looked on with horror as her mother was known to be loud and often an embarrassment to her children.

The piano player stopped, and we all quit singing. "What's going on?" asked Mr. Stark.

"The guy, the one who plays The Beast, the one who's been spending so much time with my daughter—" She paused.

"Can we help you, Mrs. Hanson?" Mr. Stark asked.

"He's been calling her and showing up at our house, so I looked him up online, and he's—" She paused again.

65

I looked at Carl, but he didn't make eye contact. He was staring at his shoes. "We really need to rehearse now, Mrs. Hanson. Can we talk about this later . . . in private?" asked Mr. Stark.

"He's a registered sex offender," she blurted out. "He needs to quit the play. We can't have him playing The Beast. We can't have him around children," she shouted.

"Oh, my God! Is this real?" asked Tess Scholberg.

"It's real. I have the paperwork to prove it. He's a danger to our children, a danger to the whole town. He needs to quit the play!"

"I second that!" screamed Tess Scholberg. "This is horrible! How could you? How could you?" she shouted at Carl.

"Give me a chance to explain. It's not what you think," Carl pleaded.

"I don't want an explanation. We trusted you with our kids," shouted Ida Johnson.

"You ruined everything! Now what will we do?" yelled Mark Davis.

"Just let me explain," said Carl.

"No! No! You dirty excuse for a human being. I want you off the play!" shouted Mark Davis, red-faced and furious.

"Is this true, Carl?" asked Mr. Stark.

"Technically yes, but . . ." Carl started.

"We want you out, you filthy piece of shit!" screamed Wesley Adler.

"I can't believe I trusted you!" shouted Mr. Stark. "You fooled us all!"

I stood there and watched as the mob mentality took over. "Fire The Beast! Fire The Beast!" they chanted. No one noticed me standing silent in the back.

Carl ran down the stairs and into the seating area to retrieve his backpack. He nervously fumbled through the books inside and found the folder for the play, took out the director's copy of sheet music, and threw it in the air in front of him. "I can't believe you're not even going to hear my side of the story! A man needs a chance to explain himself!" he shouted, but the mob was louder.

Earlier in practice, Mr. Stark had given orders for the townspeople to act more enraged, but we couldn't do it. "Really shout about how much you hate The Beast," he had said. "Take all the anger you have inside of you and release it into the scene," he directed. We tried but fell short of his vision.

I stood there and watched Carl run out of the room and wondered if this was what Mr. Stark had in mind.

"Good! We don't need his kind around here," shouted Mark Davis.

"What are we going to do now? Who's going to play the part of The Beast?" asked Linda Rudy.

"We'll figure that out. I'm just glad he's gone," said Mark.

* * *

That night I decided to go to Carl's house. I wanted to hear his side of the story, and I felt guilty for standing frozen while the auditorium descended on him. I had never been inside his house. Since I had my own apartment, we always spent time there, but he had driven past it once and pointed it out. I remembered the house because it was right on the corner of 3rd and Sunny Way, and its dark goldenrod color reminded me of a harvest sunset.

I parked on the street and nervously made my way to the door. A white-haired woman answered. "Hi. I'm a friend of Carl's. Is he here?"

She had a concerned look on her face and bit her lower lip a little before saying, "He's in the basement." She backed away from the door and motioned for me to come in. I followed her through a mismatched living room, and she pointed to the steps.

I took the steps to the basement, and there he was. He wore old gym shorts and no shirt and seemed to be frantically going through his things. "Carl," I said. "I need to talk to you."

"I don't think we have anything to say. How could you just stand there today? I waited for you in the parking lot, and you never came. How could you just stand there while those people went nuts on me?"

"I was in shock."

"*You* were in shock? How the hell do you think I felt? I hate this town. You're all nuts!"

"Can we just talk a little? Will you just sit down and talk to me?"

"I'm pretty busy right now," he said and pulled a large suitcase out from under the bed.

"What are you doing? Just talk to me!"

"Fine. You want to talk now? Fine. We'll talk," he said. I sat down on an old armchair, and he rummaged through a box by the bed and pulled out a shirt. "No one gave me a chance to say anything this afternoon, but now you wanna talk. This is so typical." He pulled a white t-shirt over his head. "When I was nineteen my friends and I got real drunk. We started daring each other to do stuff. I dared one guy to bust up a mailbox. Someone dared another guy to put cat shit in someone's mailbox, and they dared me to streak across the football field of our old high school. It was real late, like past midnight, so I did it." He went over to the dresser and started emptying the contents into boxes. "Apparently some lady in a house right by the school saw and called the cops because, before I knew it, there they were. One God-damned lady saw my ass, and I was a criminal. It was all just a joke . . . only a joke, and now I can't teach . . . I can't live anywhere without registering . . . I can't—"

"It'll be fine. We'll explain everything. They'll understand."

"Ha! You've gotta be kidding me! You think I'm going back there? Back to the lion's den? That's not happening," he yelled.

"So are you moving out of town? Why are you packing all your stuff?"

"Damn right I'm moving! These people don't have time for me, so I don't have time for them."

"You're just gonna throw it all away because of a few crazy theater people?"

"Yep," he said with contempt in his voice.

"So that's it? What about us?"

"I think you showed me enough about us this afternoon . . . I'm done," he said.

I felt my eyes welling up with tears, and he didn't even look at me as he sorted through socks before throwing them in a box. I stood there for a minute but said nothing, and then I dashed up the stairs and through the house to the security of my waiting car.

* * *

Mr. Stark ended up playing the role of The Beast. It was the logical choice since he knew all the lines, and the other actors were comfortable enough in their scenes to get through without the constant presence of a director.

I settled back into the routine of my job, more focused than ever, and I told myself that thirty-two isn't a bad age to still be single. I paid close attention to stories about women in their late thirties and even forties who were married for the first time, and I felt momentarily relaxed. But the fear crept back up when I surveyed my past relationships. The list was not encouraging. There was Tony, the guy I met online who never wanted to introduce me to his friends; Seth, the paranoid pot-head who only dated me for three weeks and probably just to have someone "normal" to introduce to his parents when they visited from out of state; Ken, the one who turned out to be gay; Steve, the guy who only called me after midnight and always wanted to get drunk and have sex; and Carl, the guy I fell in love with who fled town after being exposed as a registered sex offender.

The Contest

"Are you really going up against Bozeman?" Steve asked me. We had been sitting at the kitchen table contemplating my decision to take on Bozeman in a spicy chicken wing eating contest. "He's too strong, man. You won't have a chance," he said.

"I just need the right strategy," I said.

"Strategy? Are we talking about the same person?" he asked.

"I'm a firm believer that, if you know the right way to do something, anything is possible."

"But this is a guy who ate a foot-long sub in two bites," he said.

"Yes, and that was a glorious day, but think of the glory if I somehow win."

"You can't."

"I will," I said and immediately felt sweat beads forming on my forehead. I knew it wouldn't happen. This was a guy who could finish off four tremendous twelve meals at Perkins—a ridiculously portioned breakfast of three eggs, three pancakes, three strips of bacon, and three sausage links—and he could still eat dessert. I could barely keep two of the meals down on a good day, and poor Harvey threw up once, right there in the booth, just before finishing one, causing us to leave the money on the table before the bill came and run out of the restaurant. We didn't go back for months. Harvey and I were weak, but Bozeman was unstoppable. He once ate a gallon of peanut butter cup ice cream after finishing a 21 oz. steak dinner. I looked down at my slender body and sighed, feeling the hopelessness an old man must experience when told he is too old to drive. I could picture Bozeman blowing by me, unaffected by the food rapidly entering his mouth, and could see him pushing far ahead of my pathetic attempt to keep up.

"You won't," Steve said.

"But I'll try," I said, knowing I had to. The loser had to let the winner cut his hair, and a scissors in the hands of Bozeman scared me.

"Fine," he said. "Go ahead and try, but you're only going to be disappointed."

* * *

The next day at school I spoke to my twenty-six-year-old English teacher, "I need a good strategy to beat Bozeman in an eating contest. What have you got?"

Mr. Riggs was a high school student's dream. The parents and principal were under the impression that we spent our hour a day learning how to properly structure a research paper or going over boring grammatical rules for future use, but Mr. Riggs, whom we all called Chad, showed us tapes of *The Simpsons* most days or told stories about girls he dated or pranks he pulled with his friends growing up. "A strategy?" he said. "You came to the right guy. I beat out a 320-pound food-eating pro in a beef jerky contest, so listen closely." I smiled and sat back in the chair by his desk while the rest of the students watched Homer eat cheese.

"All you have to do is eat nothing for twenty-four hours before the contest starting point," he said, and I wondered if I should be taking notes. "Then, an hour before, drink a gallon of water. This will expand your stomach. Pee as much as you can the hour before the contest so your stomach will be empty again. During the contest, eat as fast as is humanly possible so your body doesn't realize how much you're taking in. It's a sure thing then. You'll win."

I felt my confidence rise a bit, knowing I had made the right choice picking Mr. Riggs as my mentor. I looked at him and said, "You really think I can take on Bozeman with this tactic?"

"With these tips, you can take on a giant," he said, and, for a moment, I felt a glint of hope.

"Bozeman won't know what hit him," I said.

* * *

Walking home from school that day, I concentrated hard on the mental aspect of what I was getting into; I knew I had to become one with the chicken wings, that I needed to make them a part of what was happening in my mind before they could become a part of my body. I pictured Bozeman, his amazing capacity for food consumption, his huge frame that stood tall like an empty refrigerator ready to be stocked full with chicken wings. I pictured myself as having that same capacity, as taking in more and more wings without feeling the effect of their presence inside me.

People passed, but I ignored them and kept my focus on the important matter, which they held no part in. The only characters on that day would be Bozeman and me. I dreamed of the underdog somehow pulling ahead.

* * *

"This is it," Steve said with a huge grin of anticipation on his face.

"I did everything Chad told me to do," I said. "If this doesn't grant me a victory then Bozeman really is too strong."

"It's highly possible," Steve said, and he raised one eyebrow at me.

I heard a knock on the door and took a huge breath before allowing my competitor to enter. Bozeman brought with him seven guys ready to cheer on their hero, and I felt my stomach sink as they entered.

"Bozeman," I said and shook his hand.

"Mr. Nelson, I hope you're ready for this," he said.

"I guess we'll find out," I said.

"I ate a huge Chinese buffet about two hours ago, but you know me—it shouldn't even make a dent in what I can do," Bozeman said.

A buffet? I couldn't believe what I was hearing. Bozeman may have possessed abilities others only dream of, but to go out and eat all he could only two hours before the moment of truth seemed too much.

We entered the kitchen, and Steve had a huge trough of wings in the middle of the table with a plate on each side for the bones of evidence to rest on. There were also two huge glasses of water with a pitcher in the middle in case refills were necessary.

I looked at the clock—6:26, and I sat down while focusing on breathing steadily and reminding myself of the appetite I should have possessed after going a full day without any form of nourishment.

The seven guys all patted Bozeman on the back, calling him names like Chief, Tiger, and the Conductor on the Train of Food, and they looked at me with the pity one has for a child having trouble with reading skills.

I wanted to back out, to admit this was out of my league, to run screaming from the scene and hide in my car in some unknown parking lot, but, of course, I stayed.

The four minutes passed, and Steve shot me one more glance of desperation. I knew he wanted to be over with the others on Bozeman's side of the table, but, like a proud parent of a losing little league baseball team, he remained with me.

Bozeman looked over and smiled at me confidently as I forced my eyes back down on the chicken wings before me. I swallowed hard and watched as the last seconds on the clock ticked by and started the contest that would either completely rob me of my pride or instill a self confidence in me that nothing could take away.

Bozeman's ravenous mouth met the wing in his hand, and his speed and precision were comparable to nothing. I reluctantly picked up my first wing and finished it with a steady pace before picking up the next one. We had thirty minutes to consume as many wings as possible, so I tried not to let his three-wing lead after thirty seconds discourage me or distract me from the goal at hand.

I consumed like never before, taking in wing after wing. Steve looked at me after four minutes and said, "That's ten," and I pushed onward with an effort I had never exerted before, knowing that day would make all the difference.

Bozeman's speed remained steady, but I started to ignore his performance and paid attention only to my own. It was a necessary transformation in order to gain the state of mind needed to win.

At the fifteen minute point, I had taken down thirty-two wings, and Bozeman remained ahead with his thirty-six. Then something unexpected but desperately hoped for occurred. Bozeman put his elbow on the table and rested his head against his palm while taking labored breaths and sighing in pain. I continued to eat, not yet feeling the effects of the intake, while he struggled to find a place for the extra calories amongst a stomach full of Chinese food and, most likely, a huge breakfast.

At the twenty minute mark, Bozeman only had thirty-nine bones on his plate while mine housed forty-four. I was beginning to slow down but was still not in a painful state while he cringed with every bite. Three of Bozeman's cheerleaders had moved to my side and were even calling me Chief. I felt like a god while watching him writhe in pain as I continued to take in wing after wing.

The contest ended with Bozeman's head on the table after finishing forty-two wings and my arms up in excitement and shock after successfully eating forty-nine and beating out the former king of eating contests.

* * *

I didn't eat for the remainder of the day or half the day after but heard Bozeman had gone out for pie and ice cream later that night to make himself feel better for not only losing the contest and his hair but for losing the part of him that he was most proud of. I felt a hint of loss too in gaining an awareness of his humanness, in seeing my hero fail. It was as if Christmas had still come and gone, but I had witnessed my mother filling stockings for the first time. I still had the reward, but the magic was gone.

Main Street Grind

I heard the phone ring, looked at the green blinking seven on my alarm clock, and burrowed beneath my yellow blanket, deciding not to answer. Unfortunately, my roommate, Micah's, voice from the other room betrayed my plan. "Yeah, she's home. Just a minute . . . I'll go get her."

He crept into my room, and I poked my head out to whisper, "Is that Janie? Why did you tell her I'm home? You know I avoid her calls when she calls me seven hours before my shift is supposed to start."

He handed me the phone and mouthed the word sorry.

"Hello," I said.

"Hi, Brooke. This is Janie from Main Street Grind, and I was just calling to say that I'm going to have you go ahead and come in around eight because I'm expecting a large crowd this morning."

"Eight o'clock?" I said.

"So I'll see you then?" she said in the annoying manner she had of spitting out words almost too quickly for them to be processed.

"Yeah, sure. I'll be there at eight," I said and threw the phone across the room at Micah. "I can't believe you woke me up. Now I have to go into work early and get pushed around by Janie all morning."

Micah usually worked the overnight shift at the gas station, so he wasn't home when Janie's habitual calls came at seven a.m. After the first couple, I had learned not to answer the phone, and I would wait until about one to call her back with an excuse about where I was when she called. My shift started at two, so this strategy would get me out of going in early.

* * *

Main Street Grind sat right in the middle of downtown Westfall with a green canopy over the door and two benches in front of the entrance. I had grown to hate those benches because Janie, the owner, had made me clean them every afternoon, and she always managed to find a speck of dirt somewhere in order to criticize my work. Maroon carpet and green tabletops colored the coffee shop, but the real essence of the place existed in the people.

After working there for a few months, I had memorized the drinks of the regulars and also learned details about their lives. There was Jeff, the forty-year-old man who always talked about how hard it was to get over the divorce he had experienced ten years ago; Roy, the retired man who had met a woman on the internet and was planning to marry her; George, the crabby elderly man who never said anything and simply gestured by holding up his cup when he was in need of a refill; and Edith, the sixty-year-old woman who worked at the craft store across the street and came in every morning to get a small decaf to go. These were only a few of the faces I saw every day that summer.

The owner, Janie, had seemed like a kind woman during my interview, always smiling as I answered questions and nodding her head with an eager enthusiasm as we talked. Her short gray hair and small frame made her appear non-threatening, but I soon learned that Janie had two moods—extremely sweet and overly bitchy—and, as a worker, I usually saw the negative side of her.

* * *

I walked in through the back door at 7:55 and signed my time sheet before putting on an apron. "Good morning, Charlotte," I said to the cute girl with bleached blonde hair and an adorable smile who worked with me there.

"I can't believe Janie called you to come in early. We're not even going to be busy today."

"I can," I said and smiled at her.

We spent the morning cutting up lettuce, tomatoes, carrots, lemons, and celery for lunch and intermittently waiting on people who trickled in. Janie flew through the place with a determination not necessary for the relaxed atmosphere presenting itself. "Charlotte, I thought I told you to cut up twice the amount of lettuce today for salads. Lunch is going to be a zoo."

"I'm working on it, Janie," Charlotte said.

"Why are the people at table two drinking out of to-go cups?" Janie asked as she pushed her glasses back up against her bony face.

"They asked for them," I said.

"Very good. Very good," she said and left us to do our task.

"Brooke," Charlotte said in an almost whisper.

"Yeah?"

"Don't tell Janie this, but I'm thinking about quitting."

"Why?"

"I can't take it anymore. All she does is yell at me all day long and second-guess everything I do. I've been here for a year, and I honestly feel like I know the job better than she does. She never actually does anything, just runs around and freaks out about what we're doing. Also, I got offered a job somewhere else."

I started picturing Charlotte sitting at a desk somewhere and earning a decent income. I envisioned her son wearing clothes that had been washed recently and weren't from a garage sale. "Where?" I asked.

"The snack bar in Walmart," she said with a nod that indicated I was supposed to be proud of her.

"That's great. I'm sure it will be a lot better than this."

"It will. They pay twenty cents more an hour, and you even get breaks there."

"What are you going to tell Janie?" I asked.

"I don't think I can actually tell her. Dustin tried to quit once, and Janie took him back to the kitchen and started yelling at him so much that he decided to stay. She accused him of running her business into the ground if he quit."

"Really?" I said. Dustin was the only other employee there. Janie called him the manager, but he didn't get any special benefits outside of a fifty cent raise and a lot more headaches to deal with. "So are you just going to stop showing up?" I asked.

"Well, I have to give her my key somehow, so I think I might leave a note."

"When are you going to do this?"

"The snack bar wants me to start next week sometime, so I think I'll do it today."

"I can just imagine the look on her face when she sees that," I said.

"I'm sorry," Charlotte said. "It's not going to be pretty for you."

"It's not like it is now anyway."

"Yeah, I can't believe Janie is going to have you cooking on Sundays now," Charlotte said.

"What? I never heard anything about that."

"She told Dustin and me that you were going to be the new cook for Sunday brunches since Dustin can't work weekends anymore."

"She never asked me about that, and I don't know how to cook anyway."

"Maybe I heard wrong," Charlotte said.

I had been working seven days a week and putting in about sixty hours. Since it was a small business, Janie wasn't required to pay overtime, and losing my summer and my sanity wasn't worth the pitiful increase in my pay check. I pretended the lemons were Janie's hands and cut them with more aggression than before.

"Charlotte, would you run to Central Market for me and pick up some more lettuce?" Janie said from the doorframe to the kitchen.

"I'm on it," Charlotte said, probably happy to have some time away from the tension-filled environment that Janie always created.

"So Charlotte said that you were planning on having me cook on Sundays now," I said in a weak voice.

"Excuse me?"

"Charlotte said . . ."

"Yes, yes. You will be coming in at six to do some preparation work. It's not what I would call cooking. You'll just be whipping up the quiches, French toast, roast beef, and other brunch items. It's as easy as can be. A monkey could do this. Don't worry. You'll be fine." I wondered what kind of monkey she was talking about as I turned back to the bowl of lemons.

When Charlotte returned, somewhat refreshed from her ten minute escape, I motioned for her to come to me. "You were right. She is going to start scheduling me as a cook on Sundays, and she made it look like I was worried about not being capable of doing the job instead of just not wanting extra hours here and less sleep."

"Of course she did," Charlotte said and tucked her hair behind her ears before running water for dishes.

The rest of the morning crept along, and the lunch rush Janie had predicted never came. We fed eleven people over three hours, one of the slowest lunch periods since I had started there. When two o'clock came, Charlotte took off her apron and pulled a pad of paper from her purse. Janie had run home to get some Tylenol, so Charlotte had time to compose the note. She wrote, *Sorry, Janie. I quit. I feel I can't ever do anything right. —Charlotte.* She put the note on top of the phone book, a place Janie would see but not immediately, and she put the key to the front door on top of the note. She took a final look at the place and said, "Good luck" to me before bursting through the back door.

When Janie got back from her house, she found the note and started to laugh hysterically. "What's so funny?" I said while steaming milk for a latte.

"Charlotte left me a funny note. Did she tell you about this?" I shook my head no. "She's not seriously quitting. She's just being funny," she said.

"You don't think she is?" I asked.

"No, no. I have to run an errand. I'll be back in a flash," she said and flew out the door.

I chatted casually with Mary, a woman who came in every day for an iced mocha, until the phone rang," Good afternoon. Thank you for calling Main Street Grind. How may I help you?"

"Brooke . . ."

"Is that you, Charlotte? Are you crying?"

"She's crazy, Brooke. She's fucking crazy!"

"Janie?"

"She came to my house and screamed at me in front of my son. She said that I can't quit, that if I do she's going to make my life a living hell. She said I better be there tomorrow morning at six a.m. and then said I would need these as she threw the keys at me and slammed the door."

"Oh, my God," I said and looked out the window to make sure Janie's car wasn't pulling up.

"Brooke, she's a lunatic. Get out while you still can," she said through her sobs.

"You're not coming back here, right?"

"No, I'm going to have my dad go in there tomorrow and give her the keys. I don't dare do it myself."

"Understandably. I wouldn't want that confrontation again," I said.

"I don't know how you can stand it," she said.

"After this, I don't think I can."

"You're going to quit?"

"As soon as she gets back."

"She'll be totally screwed. If you quit, Dustin will get stuck with all the hours, and he's already been thinking about quitting. This will put him over the edge. She'll be left with no one," she said.

"Which is exactly what she deserves." I noticed Janie's teal colored station wagon pulling up to the building and said, "Here she comes. I have to go."

"Okay, good luck."

Janie walked through the door with an exaggerated smile on her face and said to me, "How are you doing?" in a jovial tone of voice.

"Charlotte just called," I said.

"Oh. I'll call her right back," she said and scanned the room for the appearance of eavesdroppers.

"No. She doesn't want to talk to you."

"Well, I can talk to her tomorrow then."

"She's not coming in tomorrow."

"Yes she is."

"No. She's not. She's not coming back. Why would she after you went to her house and yelled at her?"

Janie motioned for me to keep my voice down as customers leaned in to hear the conversation more clearly. "I did not yell at her. Is that what she said, that I yelled at her?"

"She was crying on the phone. You probably traumatized her kid.

Don't lie about this."

"Charlotte is an over-reactor. Haven't you noticed that yet? She'll be in tomorrow," she said and smiled, to reassure the customers more than me.

"She doesn't want to work for you anymore . . . You know what . . ." I kicked a coffee bean under the counter with my tennis shoe and paused for a moment before saying, "Neither do I. You're a really hard person to work for. I've had a lot of bosses in my day, and I got along fine with all of them until you." I felt my face getting pink and continued to talk, getting gradually louder and more confident with each passing string of words. "You shouldn't have told me when you hired me that I would be making six fifty an hour and then later say that you had made a mistake and it was supposed to be six. You yell at me all the time for stupid things, things out of my control, and walk around here just waiting for me to make any minor mistake so you can point it out to me." I noticed the customers sitting at the counter and the way Janie nervously glanced at them and then me. I couldn't believe I was quitting in such a confrontational way, and the more unreal the situation seemed the louder my voice got. "I'm so sick of you calling me all the time in the morning and asking me to come in early when my shift is supposed to start at two, and when I do come in, you don't even act appreciative but just act like it's expected of me. It's totally unfair to not give employees overtime or breaks. The working conditions here are shit." I felt a jolt run through my body as I said that and almost smiled as Janie's face grew more defeated. "I'm twenty-two years old, and I'm so tired of being treated like a five-year-old. If you want people to actually stay working here you're going to have to learn to deal with people and not use that patronizing tone you always get."

She kept looking back and forth between me and the customers sitting at the counter. She knew they were soaking up every word, memorizing the scene so that they could report it around town later that day. Then she said, "Do you at least like working afternoons here?"

"Only when you're not around," I said and looked right at her.

"Fine, I'll finish off your shift then. Give me your key."

I put the key on the counter and walked out with a confidence I hadn't felt in years. As I was getting into my car, I saw Dustin pull up in his old van and wondered what life would be like for him on the other side of that green canopy.

Sadie's Third Wedding

I'm wearing a slate-colored dress that hangs too loosely on top and stretches uncomfortably across my stomach and thighs. The first time, I wore a yellow dress with satin fabric that acted like a window to every roll of fat and even the cellulite surfaces of my ass. The second time, I wore a red dress with ruffles down the sides that widened my already stout frame, but this time seems the worst, a slate dress whose understated ugliness pushes me even further into the shadows of existence.

It is Sadie's third wedding, and she shines in a form-fitting satin gown. For the first wedding she wore a lace sheath that conjured up images of vintage romance, movies with beauties in perfect curls. She was stunning. The second wedding, she wore a ball gown and pinned back her short locks with perfect rhinestone barrettes. She was pricelessly adorable. Now she inspects herself in the mirror as I cower in a corner of the church choir room where we prepare.

"Do I look okay?" she asks her mother through a pearly white smile and girlish giggles. Her honey colored hair is half up, and curls cascade down the back of her neck and frame her face. I hate her.

"Oh, honey. You are a vision of perfection," her mother says as she grabs Sadie's shoulders and gives her a shake of reassurance. "Marlene, will you go check on the flowers and make sure the men have their boutonnieres on straight?" she says to me.

I avert my gaze as I trudge past the mirror, awkwardly balancing myself on the pointy heels Sadie picked out for me, and take one final glance at Sadie before exiting the room. I have to take small steps as I walk because I fear that the fabric will tear if I allow myself full strides. I hate dressing up. I'm a mail carrier, so I wear pants to work every day, and when I arrive home from my job the first thing I do is put on sweatpants and an oversized t-shirt. When you look like me, comfort is the top priority in clothing selection. When you look like Sadie, beauty is the deciding factor.

As I spot Seth speaking to the photographer, I remember Sadie's first husband, Chad. He was so excited as they exchanged their vows and danced in the reception room of the old golf club. She never said what went wrong but always repeated the phrase, "We just weren't a good fit." I often wondered what that meant, having never experienced a relationship myself. Now Seth has that same smile, and I wonder at what point Sadie and Chad no longer fit. Did their marriage start to feel like my dress, too tight around the middle and difficult to walk in? Did Seth feel more like the sweatpants I lounged in at night when my favorite shows lit up the TV and buttered popcorn soothed my senses?

"Hey, Mar. You clean up nice," Seth says to me, and I wonder what it would feel like to be Sadie. The first time Randy, her second husband, saw her in that ball gown with her perfect lips painted with pink, frosted lipstick he screamed, "Wow!" and half collapsed, hands to his knees, leaning over, and momentarily suffocating as he searched the air for oxygen. I know Seth will have a similar reaction, and all the guests at the wedding and random hotel guests who see Sadie at the reception and the limo driver and the cater waiters and the couples who view the photographer's sample pictures in the future will all say the same thing: "She is such a beautiful bride."

I have never been called beautiful. I went to a wedding once for a chubby, bulldog-looking woman with wide set eyes and a boxy body, and everyone kept saying, "She looks happy," and she did, and I almost said aloud, "She looks beautiful" but stopped myself, fearing that people would wonder what I knew about beauty, but she *was* beautiful. I ran into her and her husband a year ago at a Mexican restaurant by my apartment and watched them laugh and gush about the flavor of the salsa as my mother tried to talk to me about work. They must have still fit each other somehow, even after ten years of marriage.

"How's my beautiful girl?" Seth asks me.

"She's good," I reply. "She's just finishing up getting ready. She should be out soon."

"Good because the photographer is ready to get started," he says.

Sadie and I met in middle school. I was always unnoticed, and she was always sought out by boys who wanted to live out fantasies born in early adolescence with Disney princesses and by girls who wanted their status raised by merely being in the vicinity of someone so stunning. Sadie liked having me around. I was a piece of lead next to her radiating diamond. She looked even better against the backdrop of me; it was like she was selecting the color that went best with her hair and eyes. I was an accessory. She also knew she could drone on and on about her latest romantic project, and I wouldn't clutter the conversation with details of my own life. I had no life. In school I just focused on my studies and practicing my oboe, and in adult life I deliver mail at work and play in the community band two nights a week. The rest of my time is spent with my mother or in front of the TV. I am the perfect candidate for a one-way friendship. She is lucky to have found me as an adolescent; as an adult, I may have better understood her motive. Our friendship is expected now, though, and just like hundreds of people expect me to deliver their daily mail, Sadie expects me to be her friend. I never call in sick to work, and I don't know how to say no to Sadie.

Out of the corner of my eye, I see white satin sparkling from the florescent lights of the church corridor. I can't watch another man's first sight of Sadie as a bride, so I smile shyly and give Seth a half nod as I walk the other direction toward the bathroom, not quite closing the bathroom door quickly enough because, just as I begin to enter, I hear a loud, "Oh, my God! You're beautiful!" from Seth.

Then I am safe. I am sheltered from their happiness by the dull and muted tan tones of the restroom tiles. I stand alone in front of the mirror and, for the first time all day, actually look at myself. My thin brown hair was curled and pinned up only an hour and a half ago, but it is already falling flat, and some of the bobby pins are starting to undo themselves from my hair. My thin lips look ridiculous with the mauve lipstick covering them, and somehow the color accidentally transferred onto a bit of skin around the lip line, probably because my lips are so much smaller than the tube needed them to be. Sadie bought me that lipstick for my birthday last year. It came in a makeup kit with glosses and eye shadows and lip sticks, and she said to me, "You should really think about wearing makeup. It would enhance your beauty." As I look at myself now, I wonder if this is what she had in mind. My eyes are surrounded by caves of darkness and are much smaller than Sadie's; my chin is small and pointy, and my ears awkwardly extend from the sides of my head too far for my thin hair to ever cover them.

Sadie will spend the day hoping for as much attention as two-hundred guests can possibly provide, and I will spend the day in hiding, hating every moment of walking down the aisle, the one portion of the day when people will be forced to notice my existence. As soon as Sadie enters the church in her glowing gracefulness, I will be safe. No one looks at brick walls in a room filled with roses.

"There you are," she says to me as she enters the bathroom. "You should have seen the way Seth looked at me," she says. I want to tell her that I've seen it before, that Randy and Chad had the same look. I even want to tell her that it's okay; I can catch the act next time, when a future husband sees her in a different white dress and hairstyle and gushes over a new version of Sadie. Of course, I say nothing and simply nod and smile. "That's a fun dress for you," she says and touches the fabric over my shoulder. "I knew it would work out nicely."

"Yep, it fits like a glove," I say and pull the front down again, knowing that in a few seconds it will bunch up around my stomach and continue its plan to constrict my breathing.

"Come and watch us take pictures," she says. "The bridal party photos will start in an hour."

"Okay," I say and follow her.

I sit in a pew in the back of the church by myself and watch as Sadie and Seth pose over and over again in slightly different ways. I look at my bouquet of sunflowers and want to pull all the petals off so that they match the way my body looks in this drab dress. Even Sadie's bouquet, a slightly larger replica of my own, somehow looks better than mine, as though the sun from her beauty somehow nourishes even the flowers she holds.

"Marlene, have you seen the programs? I can't seem to find them." Sadie's mother stands behind me and speaks loudly.

"Yeah, they're on the table outside of the choir room. Do you want me to set them out?"

"Would you? Thanks. That would be great," she says, and I am happy to leave the sanctuary and have a task.

I am a professional wedding coordinator by now. After helping Sadie with three weddings and having to endure an almost endless discussion of bridal minutiae, I feel like I should be paid at least half of what the licensed coordinator is making. Sadie thinks I enjoy my role because I never learned how to tell pretty people the truth and because she never learned how to pay attention to plain looking people.

I set up the programs, place the guest book on a pedestal, make sure the reader has his notes, and help the groomsmen tie cans to the back of Seth's car. For a moment, I almost feel like myself. The wedding chores remind me of delivering the mail as I mechanically move from one section of the church to the next. This feeling is, of course, shattered when Sadie finds me and says, "Come on, Marlene. It's time for the bridal party pictures."

I follow her into the sanctuary and deeply dread the thirty minutes that stand before me. We get to the front, and the photographer says, "Okay, let's have all the girls stand in a row with Sadie in the middle." She smiles at the four bridesmaids, and we line up, two on each side of Sadie. "Who is the maid of honor?" she asks.

Sadie points to me, and I feel like the photographer is disappointed. The photographer gestures for me to stand next to Sadie, and I wonder why weddings aren't more like baseball. If an outfielder has a poor batting average, the coach can send in a pinch hitter for a shot to win the game, so it seems like a good idea to have a beautiful bridesmaid serve as a stand-in for the photo portion of the day in order to improve the quality of the wedding album. Of course weddings are nothing like baseball, so I am forced to smile awkwardly and try not to blink as the photographer captures image after image of Sadie standing next to her unattractive friend.

Eventually it's over, and we return to the choir room to wait for the ceremony to start. I watch as Sadie reapplies her lipstick, as though one more coat will somehow make her more beautiful, and I pull at the place where my tights have bunched around my skinny knees, trying to move them back up to my disproportionately large thighs. I tell myself that it's almost over, that soon I will be home again under my old quilt, comfortable in the confines of my single bed. Of course I know that the night will drag on and on, that I will be forced to dance with Sadie's gawky uncle and that, when the dance is over, I will stay late with her mother and carry armloads of gifts out to the van and remove the candy left behind from the hotel tables.

The pastor enters the room and says, "It's time to go. Are you ready?"

Sadie smiles and says, "I've never been more ready," and I wonder how ready she was the first two times. Everyone in the room appears happy, but suddenly I realize that I am smiling too. Maybe we are all just acting, and Sadie's life is nothing more than a collection of pretending people circled around her and performing the parts she scripted us to play. Maybe beautiful people can't handle the realness of life and quickly retreat when it shows up in their personal interactions. It makes sense then that Sadie's marriages can only survive a year or two and always end when the flaws of humanity become visible.

We line up in the hallway outside of the sanctuary, and the music starts to play. I realize it is Canon in D, the same song Sadie had for her first wedding processional. She must have decided that, like crop rotation, it was okay to repeat parts of the service as long as a wedding or two had passed in between. I wish the music was faster so I could hurry down the aisle, but, as the notes slowly settle into their places, I walk arm-in-arm with the best man leisurely while the entire congregation watches me. The song ends, and I am protected again by Sadie standing in the back of the church, ready to glide confidently down an aisle of adoration.

I watch Seth watch her and wonder what her next dress will look like. During the ceremony, my mind keeps wandering—I've seen this all before—and I keep thinking about the happy bride, the bulldog faced one, the one whose smile was luminous as she gazed back and forth between her overweight groom and the faces of friends before her. Sadie is beautiful, but she was real. As the pastor concludes the ceremony and Sadie kisses Seth, I close my eyes for a second and try to imagine what it would feel like to be the bride who was loved for nothing more than living the life she created.

The Hypothesis

It was supposed to be a glorious day. That was the plan, but something happened, something unexpected and severely disappointing.

I was one of eight men on a mission to prove the hypothesis, but Bozeman and Harvey were the ones who would carry out the experiment. We couldn't have guessed that one of them would fail when we chose them, but after it happened, it seemed that the outcome was obvious all along.

We arrived at McDonald's around six p.m. and sat in the car to work it all out before entering. A week before, Bozeman had spoken enthusiastically about the benefits of the double stack, a signature sandwich at Wendy's. The sandwich could be purchased for a meager price of 99 cents, but the experience of such a masterpiece of meat was worth far more. Bozeman declared that the double stack was never a bad idea, stating that if a person was anywhere within a mile radius of Wendy's it would *always* be beneficial to drop in and enjoy the economical and flavorful joys associated with the double stack. He smiled knowingly and said, "It's like if you see a five dollar bill on the ground. It doesn't matter if you're rich or have no money at all; you're always going to bend down and pick it up. The same is true of the double stack. You could be hungry or extremely full, and it would still be a good idea." Of course, proving that a hungry person would be better off was easy. It was the latter part of the theory that needed testing, so on that Saturday evening we set out to do just that.

The plan was for Bozeman and Harvey to eat as many hamburgers at McDonald's as possible and then head over to Wendy's and order the double stack, triumphantly finish it, and prove its importance. I carried the camera to record the event while the other guys cheered on the testers of the hypothesis, Bozeman and Harvey.

"This is going to be the best day of our lives," said Harvey as he waited at the counter for his three hamburgers to be placed on the tray.

"Are you sure you're the man for the job?" I asked.

"No question," he said.

The hamburgers came, three to Harvey and five to Bozeman, and we took our seats as I snapped two pictures of the guys before the truth was known.

Bozeman ate his like he had been in the jungle for weeks and was rediscovering food, but Harvey's process was not as smooth, and by the end it looked like each bite was more agonizing than the last. We clapped while chanting his name as the other restaurant goers looked on in a mixture of confusion and annoyance.

The drive to Wendy's was a crucial moment as Bozeman's spirits rose, and Harvey tried to gain some confidence from the support we offered up. I drove aggressively, knowing that every minute before Harvey got the sandwich would be a disadvantage; we couldn't allow his stomach to get very far in the digestion process. All the other drivers who displayed anger by my sloppy methods of passing and close calls with yellow lights didn't realize what was at stake.

Upon arrival, we burst through the doors and managed to get the sandwiches quickly.

"This is going to be the best day of our lives," I said but more to prove it to myself than to display confidence.

"Harvey, are you going to puke?" one of the guys asked.

"No, he's going to be fine," I said, knowing that a loss of the food would be a disqualifier. I took another picture as they each took the first bite, and I hoped the lights had a green tint and that Harvey wasn't as sick as he looked.

Things appeared to be going along as anticipated. They were each almost half done, and Bozeman was moving steadily as Harvey's chewing remained forced. Bozeman pulled ahead and amazingly took the last half in only two bites while throwing his hands up and screaming at the top of his lungs, "I am God!" We all huddled around him, hugged him, and felt, for a moment, the pure feeling of victory. In our celebration, we almost forgot the real question: could Harvey pull it off?

He couldn't. He picked up the remaining third of the sandwich and stomped out of the restaurant while we followed and watched him throw the double stack on the ground in the parking lot and step on it. He was broken. Bozeman had become a man that day while Harvey remained behind, standing in the midst of his own disappointment and having to deal with the reality of letting the whole team down too.

We drove away in silence and got about two miles from Wendy's before Harvey spoke. "Go back," he said.

"What?" I asked.

"I'm going to do it. Go back," he said.

"But . . ."

"Please," he said in desperation, so I drove.

We stayed in the van as he got out, and we watched him pick up the disfigured double stack from the parking lot. He took one bite and then another, but in the end he failed, and there was nothing we could do. We blamed it on the dirt and motor oil that had altered the flavor, but I know it didn't comfort him. The truth couldn't be changed.

Why I Changed My Major

Dr. Stockhousen didn't look like he had earlier that day as he slowly made his way through the living room to get a drink from the kitchen. His torn jeans and dark brown sweater resembled my friend, Philip's, and he wore old black tennis shoes instead of wing tips.

I found a comfortable sofa and took out the staff paper with my composition neatly printed in pencil on it. He returned and smiled at me before saying, "They should be here any minute. Can I get you anything to drink?"

"No thanks. I'm fine," I said, crossed my legs, and tapped my left foot in six-eight time, letting the piece weave through my thoughts before hearing it played for the first time.

We were required to write different styles of music—sonatas, fugues, jazz charts, and minuets—for our music composition course, and I, being an overly ambitious student, chose to take the course my freshman year. After we finished a piece, we had to choose musicians from class who played the instruments we wrote for and have them rehearse and play it for the class. Dr. Stockhousen let students use his home for practice space.

"I told them to be here at seven," I said. "I don't understand why they're not here yet."

"Some people don't take school as seriously as they should. That's why I like you, Chloe. You understand the importance of things like effort and punctuality," he said and took a sip of his orange juice with a shot of vodka.

We heard a knock on the door followed by the bell, and he abruptly put down his glass to answer it.

Katie seemed to fall into the room with her tuba case that weighed almost as much as her small body, and she immediately asked, "Dr.

Stockhousen, what do you have to drink?"

"Let's see," he started. "I can make you a rum and coke or a screw-driver, or you can have a beer."

"I'll have that orange juice thing I had last time," she said.

"Screwdriver it is. You sure you don't want a drink, Chloe or just some water?"

"No, thanks. I'm fine," I said.

Marlene and Matt arrived together a few minutes later, and the three players took out their instruments—tuba, oboe, and bassoon. Dr. Stockhousen had given me a quirky smile when I originally asked his opinion of my instrument combination and said, "Nontraditional—I like that, Chloe."

I handed them each their transposed copy and set the score out on the coffee table in front of me, and we started running through it. The fugue I heard them play differed drastically from the ideal copy in my head. Their amateur ears could not detect the syncopation in the second measure of each part's lead in, and the tuba was ten cents sharp in correlation to the oboe and bassoon. I looked at Dr. Stockhousen, and he knew. He sensed the real music and the great discrepancy between that and what those three were playing. He saw their interpretation for what it was—a failed attempt to reproduce something great.

After three times through, he looked at them and said, "That will do. I think the class will get a good idea of Chloe's piece from our session here. Thanks for stopping by." I put the sheet music back into my red folder and picked up my backpack to go. "Chloe, could you stay for a minute more so we can discuss your thoughts on this?" he asked.

While I watched the others carelessly put their instruments away without cleaning them, I looked at him and said, "Sure."

We sat in silence until they left and we were safe to say our true thoughts on the situation. "Went pretty well, didn't it?" he said after Matt closed the door behind the three of them.

"Pretty well? Katie's tuba was sharp the whole time. The dotted sixteenth notes were atrocious. Does Marlene ever clean that oboe after rehearsal? Maybe that's why it sounds so cloudy. I could have gotten a better sound on an oboe, and it's nothing like my trombone."

"You care more than they do," he said and moved from the chair to sit by me on the dark blue velvet couch. "To them this is a nuisance, stopping here to practice, practicing at all. They're just waiting to get on with their lives. Life for them takes place outside of the music," he said.

"Life for me is the music," I said.

"I know."

"Remember when you gave us those CDs to listen to, the ones of the pieces we were going to go over in class the next week?"

"Yeah," he said.

"I fell asleep listening to one of them. I took it with me in the car and listened to it on my way to work and home, put it on my iPod to listen to during my science lecture, and couldn't get anything done for two days because it completely took my attention. I don't know the meaning of background music. It doesn't matter what it is, any genre, it always has my attention. Even that night when I fell asleep I might not have been technically sleeping; the music seeped into me and made my dreams musical. I know it sounds crazy, but that's how it is for me," I said.

"No. That's as it should be. Music should be an experience, not a chore," he said and nodded to me.

His dark hair never moved. It was tied back in a ponytail all the time and usually held in place by dirt and oil. I had noticed that semester that he showered only on Mondays and that, as the week wore on, his hair grew dirtier and his facial hair longer. I was glad it was only Wednesday.

"Have you always loved music?" I asked, immediately realizing the pointlessness of such a question.

"Of course," he said and scratched his bare knee through the hole in his jeans.

"Well, thanks for helping me with this project. It was really nice to let us meet at your house."

"Chloe, being a professor gets lonely," he said. "When you're a student you can hang around other students, but as a professor, who do I have?"

"Other professors, I guess," I answered and took my purse. "Well, thanks again, but I should get that theory assignment you gave us done, and it's getting late. You know how I am. I hate to put things off."

"You can have an extension," he said. "Just stay and visit a while."

Finding no obvious excuse, I said, "I suppose I could" and sat back down.

"You see, it's weird for me because I'm only thirty-four, but students seem to look at me like I'm an old man."

"I don't, Dr. Stockhousen," I said.

"Ted. Call me Ted."

"Okay . . . Ted." We sat in silent awkwardness for a while as I searched for something substantial to say, but the conversational void didn't seem to disturb him. Finally, I said, "So what do you do when you're not at school?"

"There's something you should hear," he said and got up to put a CD in. "It's music you can see," he said and threw the CD case on the couch beside me.

"What is it?" I asked.

"It's Pink Floyd, a song called 'Any Color You Like.'" He picked up the case and sat back down, much too close. I was on the end of the couch, and he was half on the same cushion as me and half on the edge of the middle one. There wasn't much room for me to work with, so I inched over to the very end and tried to balance my body with part of it hanging off beyond the armrest. "What do you think?" he asked.

"It's really good."

"No. It's fucking amazing," he said, and I noticed him looking straight at me.

Without turning toward him, I said, "Maybe I should go now. The song is really great, but . . ."

He shook his head at me and pointed at the stereo. "You have to hear the rest of this. Trust me."

I listened as the tempo increased and the volume rose, and the notes slipped smoothly into each other. "Chloe, can't you feel that the whole world is in this—these notes, this guitar, this room?" He grabbed my face and turned it toward him, and he kissed me with the same awkward rhythm the student musicians had displayed. I listened to the pulsating drum beats and chaotic synthesizer flailing above the guitar solo, and as the song slowed and approached the resolution of the last chord I got up to leave.

The next day I changed my major.

The Healer

"Arise. Face the morning light. Life is waiting for you on the other side of these walls," chanted Samuel Thunder. I stared at our leader, a white man in tan moccasins that were probably purchased at the local Shoe Mart. His light brown hair hung in loose braids that fell casually down his bare back, and his expression was distant as he stared hard at a portrait of a Native American man standing next to a bison. In the three months I had been attending the sessions, I had often noticed him fixated on this painting as though he could somehow transfer some of the paint from this imagined man's skin onto his own pale flesh.

I guessed we were about ten minutes into the session, but there were no clocks in the meditation room. Samuel Thunder said awareness of time was the thief of self development, that we had to be willing to let time pass without knowing how much in order to find our true passion. If we could become so advanced in this method so as to live life unaware of our age then we could hold onto our youth forever.

"Let yourself fall into the nothing of wordlessness," he said, and he started droning on mostly the same note with only the occasional break for a long inhale. His face contorted awkwardly as he struggled to stay motivated through the exercise. This seemed to last about twenty minutes, but there was no way to know. I felt myself fighting the urge to pull the watch out of my pocket and see how much of the two hour session remained.

On my first visit, I had made the mistake of assuming, "Arise. Face the morning light. Life is waiting for you on the other side of these walls" was a declaration that it was time to leave. This was not the case. It was merely part of what Thunder called "the visualization process." He said that, in

99

any given situation, your mind must prepare for arrival or departure four times. The next session, I heard the phrase four times and assumed the fourth time indicated the end of the session. I was wrong. I eventually became frustrated with trying to find the pattern, and I arrived at the conclusion that either Thunder was trying to teach us about the random nature of life or that he had just lost count.

Eight of us stood in two rows of four in the small meditation room. The walls were painted dark brown, and the carpet was just a shade lighter. The only decoration, besides the painting, came in the form of a few words painted in white at eye level along the walls: "Spirit," "Desire," "Atmosphere," "Separation," "Substance," and "Humanity." I had no idea why the words were there. After eleven sessions, I still couldn't figure out their significance. Maybe that was intentional, or maybe they were just remnants from the leader who had used the room before Thunder. We weren't allowed to talk to him, so there was no way to know.

I started coming to the sessions after my apartment building burned down. A neighbor fell asleep with a cigarette in her mouth, and I lost all my possessions as well as the ability to sleep through the night with a sense of safety. The flier promised that Thunder could instill total tranquility and confidence in just twenty sessions for only $2,500. I was more than halfway through the program and still had nightmares.

We were instructed to come in comfortable clothes, so I wore old sweat pants and an oversized t-shirt. Shoes were to be removed before entering, so the row of sandalwood candles sitting on the side table had to work hard to fight the scent of sweaty summer feet. As Thunder leaned forward and extended his arms straight out in front of him, we all imitated the motion. He staggered when clients started the class so that there were always a few followers who knew the routine and could show the newcomers what to do. When Thunder positioned his body, we knew to do the same, and when he repeated a word or phrase three times in a row, we knew to chime in for the fourth time.

He stood straight again and said, "You must not notice your neighbor. Pay attention only to your own hands, your own presence." I couldn't help but notice the hands of the man next to me as Thunder lifted his thin hands above his head and spread his bony fingers apart. The man next to me had dirt lodged into the creases of his palms. It was his first time, and he didn't seem to fit in with the room of people who were obviously beaten down by life. There was Betty, the fifth grade teacher who had recently discovered a strong hatred toward children; Glenda, the toll booth worker who had just found her husband in bed with a friend from church; and Nathan, the college student who struggled with severe OCD. The only person who remained from my first session was Laurie, the rare coin distributor who had recently quit her job after finding out that the buffalo nickels her company sold were fabricated. She always stood beside me, and I sometimes noticed her looking at the bison painting and wondered if it was a painful distraction for her. The newcomer, with his strong square jaw and solid body, almost resembled the man in the painting. I pictured him chasing bison on the wild plains of Western Nebraska and stabbing them with a sharp spear, and I suddenly realized that the man who so patiently listened to Thunder's wisdom was himself more real than the man who led the session. Maybe this was why he wanted us to focus only on ourselves; it made him seem more powerful if we weren't allowed to compare him to the others.

I always left feeling discouraged and unsure whether or not I would return the next week, but every Tuesday night I drove from my job at the phone company to the motel room I was temporarily staying in, grabbed a granola bar and coke, and rushed to the other side of Minneapolis to be there by seven. More than anything else, it was the money that kept me going back. I had invested so much that I couldn't justify quitting.

"Stand tall like the oak that lives on wild expanses beyond the city walls," Thunder said, and we all stretched our torsos and puffed out our chests. Three months ago, after my first session, I tried to incorporate this lesson into my daily life, but using perfect posture, as I moved around the office from my desk to the copy machine and back again, only made me feel self-conscious.

"Breathe the scent of the earth. Let it soothe your bones and slow your blood," he said, and I wondered if nature smelled anything like the candles that were probably manufactured in a warehouse in China. I went to a state park up in Northern Minnesota for a school field trip when I was thirteen, and I had pictures of me standing in a forest by a lake, but I couldn't remember what it smelled like.

"I am still. I am listening. I am still. I am listening. I am still. I am listening," he said, and we all joined him for the fourth time, "I am still. I am listening," we chanted. Huge portions of the sessions were spent in silence, but I didn't know what I was supposed to be listening for. Was it my inner voice? Was it answers to the questions of my life? I usually just watched him standing in front of us motionless. Sometimes I thought about the groceries I needed to buy, or I went over conversations I had had with coworkers that day. One time I tried counting to estimate how long the silent period lasted, but I got bored around a thousand and started thinking about something else.

After what must have been at least thirty minutes, he relaxed his body and slowly untied the leather strap holding his tan leather pants around his waist. "I am Samuel Thunder," he said. "Who are you?"

"Megan Green," I said as the others simultaneously stated their names, and the newcomer stood in silence.

Thunder loosened the elastic waist and removed the pants, revealing a leather loincloth. "I am Samuel Thunder, and I am not ashamed," he said. During my first session, I had to bite down hard on my lower lip to prevent the eruption of laughter I felt bubbling up inside me. I had seen pictures of sexy Native American men who could pull off this look with their muscular legs and sturdy upper bodies, but Thunder couldn't. His pale, mostly hairless legs looked even more fragile beside the small strip of leather, and the string around his waist seemed to be the same size as the collar of a half-grown dog. At my third session, there was a new member, a middle-aged man who wore an argyle sweater and corduroy pants. When Thunder got to this point, the man nervously scratched his elbow, and, after about thirty seconds, turned around and left. I watched the newcomer, but he didn't appear to be bothered.

"If I remove the clocks from this room, from this city, and from this world, if I drown out the ticking of time passing, I can stay like this forever. My body will never change," he said. As I looked at his scrawny frame, I wondered if that was the right goal for him.

Because we weren't allowed to talk to Thunder, he always entered the room right at seven and left as soon as he was through. A young woman let us in when we arrived and escorted us out at the end of the evening. One week, a woman who only came once tried to ask him a question. "What are we supposed to be learning here? How does this effect . . ."

"No!" he shouted. "Asking eliminates your process of perception." He waved his arms wildly and shook his head at her. He turned on a CD of tribal music, and we clumsily attempted to follow the repetitious dance he performed. I remember a lot of stomping and an almost violent thrusting forward of the neck muscles. The day after, I sat at work and tried to massage the pain out of my neck while hoping that no one else would ask Thunder any questions.

"Touch your skin. You are part of the earth. You are the earth." Thunder stood straight and stroked his white chest with both hands, but I focused on my peripheral vision and watched the newcomer rub the underside of his left hand with his right thumb. I felt the delicate skin just above my eyelid and wondered what time it was.

"It is up to you to tell the world who you are," he said. He picked up a wooden walking stick and, one by one, pointed it at each of us. "The world will accept you if you know yourself." I wondered who he spent his time with outside of the meditation room. "You must first know your feet before you can see with your eyes," he said and set down the stick. We all stared at our feet, and I wondered if I knew my feet yet, after eleven sessions. It seemed like only the newcomer should be focusing on his feet, and maybe the rest of us could move on to the knees, hips, or neck. I guess we were supposed to do that on our own time.

"Arise. Face the morning light. Life is waiting for you on the other side of these walls," he said and clapped his hands together, signifying the end of the session. He picked up his pants and the walking stick, turned around, and walked out the door at the front of the room. I always wished he would put on the pants first. After seeing his bony backside once during my first session, I always closed my eyes as he turned around and kept them closed until the door shut behind him.

I bent down to pick up my purse, and the newcomer turned to me and said, "This guy is brilliant."

"Yeah, he really is," I said with a smile, flung my purse over my shoulder, and headed for the door.

Outside the chaos of the city was calming and familiar, and the dingy motel room that waited for me seemed inviting and interesting with its cable television and telephone and the possibility of overhearing an argument from the couple next door. The smell of the sidewalks littered with dead leaves and trash and the sea of honking automobiles surrounded me, and I was home.

Director of Fun

It seemed like a ridiculous idea, hiring a director of fun for the new inn. "Can't people make their own fun?" I asked my sister, Margie.

"Trust me. This is better. I went to a hotel in Northern Maine a few summers ago, and they had one, and it was great," she said with a reassuring smile and a nod.

"What did this person do exactly?"

"He made suggestions of fun things to do around town," she started.

"Can't the front desk person do that?" I broke in.

"But it was more than that. He really went out of his way to ensure we were having a good time. Since the town pretty much closed shop after dinner, he stayed at the hotel and hung around the lobby singing and playing guitar, telling jokes, orchestrating games. One day it rained all afternoon, so he organized an indoor scavenger hunt for the guests who were restless. It really improved the vacation experience."

"So he was like a camp counselor for adults?"

"You might say that. He was a college kid, and adults love hanging around with young people. It makes them feel like they are still young," she said.

"So it's kind of like paying someone to be your friend?" I asked.

"Kind of . . . but the beauty of it is the indirectness of the transaction."

"What do you mean?" I asked.

"The guests aren't paying him. They would pay you to pay him, so they are unaware of the fact that they're paying someone money to hang out with them."

"But you were aware of it," I said.

"Don't worry. Most people don't think about these things so deeply, especially not when they're on vacation. Just trust me. This will improve the overall experience for your guests and make them more likely to come back," she said.

"Okay. I'll think it over," I said.

* * *

The next week I found myself interviewing for the position of director of fun. Two Harbors, Minnesota, is a small town, and most of the college-age kids leave for the summer to work in Minneapolis or at resorts and camps around the state, so I only had four applicants and interviewed two of those.

The first guy I met was Sean, a lanky twenty-year-old who lived in town during the summer and attended Lake Superior State University. He was still undecided on his major. He came in for the interview wearing a shirt and tie and khaki colored pants.

"Hi, Sean. Come have a seat," I said and wandered over to the couches in the middle of the lobby with my clipboard in hand. He followed me and seemed unsure of where to sit. "Just have a seat right here," I said and pointed at the couch across from me.

"Okay," he said and sat down.

"So why do you feel you would be a good candidate for the job of fun director?" I asked.

"Um . . . I like to have fun," he responded and looked at his shoes.

"What would you do to ensure my guests are having a good time?"

"Just talk to them and stuff," he said.

"Okay. That's good. What else?"

"I can do some magic tricks," he said and shrugged his shoulders.

"That's good. The kids would like that," I said, and I suddenly realized I didn't know how much a director of fun was supposed to be paid. It seemed like a waste of money to pay Sean much of anything when it soon became obvious that even his parents might find his personality slightly tedious.

"I guess I'm not really sure what this job is supposed to be, so it's hard to answer," he said. I wasn't sure either. I wished Margie was doing the interview. Hell, sometimes I wished Margie was the one opening the inn. She was always better at the process of making something from nothing. When we were kids, she started clubs with ease and usually had to end them because the membership got out of control and they no longer felt like clubs after losing their nature of exclusivity. Opening the inn was always my husband's dream, and when he died I decided to finally try to make a go of it.

"That's okay. I can train you if you're hired. The purpose of the interview is just for me to get a glimpse of your personality," I said.

"Okay," he said.

"What do you like to do for fun? Maybe that's a good place to start."

"I don't know. I guess I like videogames and watching movies," he said.

"Can you play any instruments?" I asked, remembering Margie's comment about the guy who entertained guests with guitar and singing.

"Nope. I played the saxophone in fifth grade, but that didn't go too well. I quit after that year."

"Do you have any experience organizing games?" I asked.

"My friends and I used to play Dungeon's and Dragons, but I was never the Dungeon Master," he said in a somewhat defeated tone.

"That's okay," I said. "The games here would be more like your typical rainy day games: chess, checkers, charades, Pictionary—that kind of stuff."

I had no idea what I was doing. I had imagined him doing most of the talking while I interjected with a question from time to time, but he just sat there, relying on me to keep the process going, and I was running out of questions. "So how do you like college?" I asked, knowing the question had nothing to do with the available job.

"It's alright," he said and shrugged his shoulders.

I dug my nails into my collarbone, a nervous habit I had formed as a child, and waited for him to say more, but he just sat there, hands folded in his lap, staring down at the travel magazines strewn across the coffee table between us. I sighed and said, "I have a few more interviews to do before deciding on the job."

"Gotcha," he said and nodded.

"Well, Sean. It was nice meeting you. I'll let you know about the job in the next couple of days," I said and stood up to shake his hand. He didn't stand with me but instead nodded and took out his phone to check for new text messages. I knew I wouldn't see him again and started to question the concept of hiring a fun director.

That question only lingered in my mind for two hours until I met Jeff, the second interviewee. Margie had met him a week earlier in the café downtown and told him about the job. She had said, "You have to meet this guy! He is the definition of a fun director. He's twenty-two, great to talk to, and looking for summer work. Trust me on this one." I called him up that day and made an appointment to meet with him after my interview with Sean.

Jeff came to the interview five minutes early and seemed to spring into the room with his lively steps and the overstated way he pushed the door open as though to ensure I would be alerted to his presence. His big blue eyes and the mop of curly blonde hair paired with his tall, stocky frame made him almost appear cartoonish, and I instantly knew he would be the one for the job.

"You must be Jeff," I said.

"Yes. The director of fun has arrived," he said and bowed in an exaggerated way as I made my way around the counter to offer a handshake.

This time I didn't have to tell him where to sit. Jeff actually led me, and the interview was the same. He told me of his extensive background of theater and music. He made jokes and sang "Mrs. Robinson" to showcase his musical ability. Toward the end of the song he sang, "Here's to you, Frances Worthington. Jesus loves you more than you will know. Oh, oh oh" and winked at me. I was actually having fun, and during the hour that Jeff sat across from me I forgot about all the work ahead of me. I forgot about the fact that the inn was only filled up for the first week and that it was mainly my relatives and friends who had booked rooms out of a sense of obligation to help my business get off the ground. I forgot about the other hotels on my street and the brutal competition of the tourist industry in my small Lake Superior town, and I even forgot that I was sixty-one and just now starting over. Talking to Jeff made me feel like I was on vacation, and, somewhere in the middle of it, I felt twenty-one again. I was just a girl talking to a boy about life. This is what I wanted my guests to feel. More than the serenity of a lakeside view, more than the fun of casual afternoons looking at souvenirs or eating pie at the local diner, more than the comfort of a king sized bed and plush towels after long showers, more than any of the details of a weekend getaway, I wanted them to feel the simple happiness of their youth. Jeff could give them that.

"It was very nice meeting you, Mrs. Worthington," he said.

"Call me Frances," I said and prepared myself to say goodbye but instead said, "You have the job. Can you start next Monday?"

"Of course. What time?" he asked.

"Is nine okay?"

"Nine's perfect," he said, and it suddenly seemed like everything was going to turn out okay.

* * *

"How's it going with Jeff?" Margie asked. The inn had been open for a month, and things were pretty slow but steady enough to almost pay the bills, so I was optimistic. Margie spent most of her time at the inn helping with housekeeping and bookkeeping, and she refused to take any wages, saying that sisters help each other out and reminding me of all the hours I spent babysitting her five children. We often stood behind the counter and watched Jeff work. It felt like watching a play as the animated aspects of his personality somehow transferred to everyone he interacted with and made them more interesting too.

"Are you kidding? He's great," I said. "I already had two guests call to book a room who mentioned hearing about Jeff from a friend who stayed here. If this continues, he'll bring in a substantial amount of business before the summer is over."

"Too bad he has to go back to school," she said.

"That's the other thing I was going to tell you about," I said. "Jeff came to me this morning and said he's going to take his sophomore year off. He needs to earn more money before going back to school, so he'll be here all year!" I said, and I could feel my face beaming as I revealed the news.

"Sophomore year? I thought he was going into his senior year. Isn't he twenty-two?" she asked.

"He's had a few setbacks, and working so hard on a music and theater career has made studying take a back seat, so he failed some classes along the way, but isn't this great, Margie? Can you even imagine how much fun this is going to be?"

"You're right. Jeff is great for business. It's amazing how people of all ages love him. I've never seen anything like it before. He might be the most likeable person I've ever met," she said.

"I know," I said. "This guy is just perfect."

* * *

The following weeks continued the trend of more people booking rooms at the inn, and we were averaging more than half capacity nearly every weekend. The first week in September we even had one Saturday night when all but three of our sixty-two rooms were full. There was a wedding in town, and most of the wedding party, along with dozens of wedding guests, chose our inn for their stay after the reception. Jeff stayed late that night and kept the party going in the lobby, and around two a.m. he moved everyone outside to the lakeside lawn behind the inn. They roasted s'mores, sang old camp songs, danced beside the dark waves of the lake, and told stories of the great adventures their lives had seen. I sat in one of the vacant rooms with the window open and listened all night to the steady sound of the waves and the laughter and music below. Around four, I heard the last of the guests trickle into the lobby and the muffled sound of voices in the hallway outside my room. I heard the door next to mine close softly and made my way down to the lobby to say goodnight to Jeff.

He was sitting on the couch just staring off into space, probably exhausted from working the seventeen hour shift of entertaining strangers. "You didn't have to stay until the end," I said as I approached him.

He seemed surprised to see me and replied, "Nah, it was fun. They were some pretty crazy people. I guess alcohol will do that, though."

"True enough," I said.

"I'm surprised you're still up," he said.

"Me too. I guess it was all the excitement of the inn being full. It feels like something is really happening here, like it's all going to work out," I said.

"Did you have doubts?"

"Of course. I pretty much jumped into this blindly. Roger, my husband, was much more suited to this sort of thing. He used to talk about it all the time. He gave me the idea, and after he died of a heart attack, I felt like I had to try this."

"I know what you mean," he said and smiled.

"Well, you should get home. It's really late, and you need to get some sleep."

"I'm not tired. I like talking to you. Maybe we can just sit here for a little while," he said, and I wondered if I would have to pay him for the extra hour of talking to me. Was I like my guests, paying for human companionship? Of course he didn't really want to talk to an old woman with white hair, deep-set wrinkles around the eyes and forehead, and lumpy legs and breasts. It was only his job.

"Sure," I said. "We can do that," and we sat there in the lobby, talking comfortably to each other. He told me about his dreams of becoming a great stage actor or running a theater program for kids. He told me how he wanted to live in each state and take summer trips to faraway places like Iceland, China, and Portugal. He revealed embarrassing details about his first breakup and how he fought for months to try to get the girl back, and he spoke of his intense fear of having children, knowing that they would change his plans and steer him down an alternate path.

I told him about a road trip I once took from Fargo to Southern Florida, something I hadn't thought about much in decades. He put his feet up on the table and rested his head back on the couch but stared straight at me with a slight smile that seemed to indicate interest, so I went on, "It's strange, but even after forty years, I can still remember drinking root beer and rolling down the windows of my friend's old Buick as we passed state lines and sang along to the radio. The smell of the ocean in my long hair seemed better that trip than it did later on when I went back. I guess that was the last time in my life that I felt free," I said and looked at Jeff.

"Getting older must be hard," he said, and somehow it didn't annoy me the way that statement did when other young people said it.

"Yeah, it's not what I expected. I used to think the problem with getting older is that you no longer recognize yourself, but it's actually the opposite. Other people no longer recognize you. It seems to be even more true for women. My white hair and wrinkles separate people from knowing me. Even the people who knew me when I was young and beautiful seemed to see me less and less as the years separated my body from the person I've always been."

He nodded at me, and I noticed the sun streaming through the wooden blinds across the lobby and looked at my watch. Somehow it was almost seven. I hadn't stayed up all night since my senior year of college, the year before I met Roger. My college boyfriend, Don, and I used to sit up all night talking about our philosophy class, music, and his painting projects. Roger was much more practical. "Sleep at night or don't sleep at all," he used to say, but sometimes I missed the feeling of braving the uninhabited hours while the rest of the world slept through them.

"I'm trying to get all the freedom I can while it's still available to me," he said. "My parents can't see that. They think I'm distracted and uncommitted, but it's really the opposite. I refuse to settle into any one thing unless I know it's worth stopping for."

"I guess the trick is to just keep driving," I said. "Even after Roger's funeral, I had this intense desire to get in my car and get away from it all, but instead I built an inn."

"Maybe this is the adventure," he said.

I didn't want to tell him the truth, that running the inn that summer was actually exciting for me, that there were moments when I felt young again, when I could feel the freedom of unexplored hours before me. I didn't want to tell him that staying up late talking to him that night gave me the kind of radiating happiness I hadn't known since college, so I just said, "Maybe so."

"Or at least you're helping other people have their adventures," he said.

"That's a good way of seeing it. Well, I need to get the morning coffee ready, and people will be starting to check out soon," I said.

"Alright. It was really nice talking," he said and stood up lazily to stretch.

"Yeah, I had a lot of fun," I said.

"We'll have to do this again sometime," he said, and I felt myself smiling more than I should have.

"Sounds good," I said and watched him leave before turning to my morning chores.

* * *

That was the last time I saw Jeff. He called in sick for his shift on Monday and never showed up for his shifts the rest of that week. I tried his number but kept getting the voicemail, and a couple of weeks later I got a letter in the mail from him stating that he had gotten an invitation to visit some friends of friends in New Orleans. He thought it would be a good opportunity to get acquainted with some local artists and musicians and learn to cook real Cajun food, he said.

I was surprised how much the inn changed after that. It was becoming more popular, rooms were full most weekends, and even weekday nights pulled in a decent profit, but the fun was gone. Margie was right. You need someone around to make sure the guests are entertained. Without that, an inn turns into nothing more than a place to get some sleep.

Fountain Friends Pen Company

"There are nights of true passion waiting for me in future hours," she whispered aloud during a dull Tuesday afternoon meeting at the Fountain Friends Pen Company where she had been employed for eight long and tedious years. She had read this in a book the night before and couldn't stop thinking about what it meant. The very idea of "true passion" confused her, and how could a character be so convinced of the unknown direction of her future?

"Did you say something, Holly?" asked Tom, the manager who made her weekly existence one that few would envy.

"Yes," she said in a slightly louder voice.

"Was it something about the new ad slogan?"

"No."

"Well? What did you say?" he asked.

She wondered if she was experiencing a break-down of some sort but repeated, "There are nights of true passion waiting for me in future hours" and started to stand up but couldn't catch her sense of balance on the new beautifully impractical high-heeled shoes. She was tired of wearing clothes she hated to work every day, tired of waking up at hours when her body desired nothing more than to burrow back beneath the cozy confines of the covers, tired of talking to dull people about dull subjects, tired of pretending to care about ad slogans and company policies, just tired.

"I don't think that slogan is going to sell pens, but you're right. Something sexy might not be a bad idea," he said.

"No. I'm not talking about the pens. I'm talking about my life," she said.

"What does your life have to do with Fountain Friends?" Tom asked.

It seemed like such a simple question, but the answer had taken eight years to compose. The truth was that Fountain Friends had nothing to do with Holly, yet it accounted for most of her waking hours for most of her adult life. She had spent an entire month doing research on the emotional effect of color in ads in order to decide what color the personified male pen's hat should be. She had stayed late at the office for three weeks drawing up countless designs for the smile on Mr. Pen's face after Tom read that a company in England lost significant revenue because their male mascot looked too feminine. She had often skipped lunches in order to negotiate ad space prices with small town newspapers, and she developed friends in order to strategically network with influential people. Even before starting the job at the pen company, she had stayed up late many nights memorizing terminology for monotonous tests in order to earn her degree.

Sitting in the meeting, she started to imagine her life outside of the office building, outside of the confines of deciding whether the newly introduced female pen should be shaking Mr. Pen's hand, hugging him, or giving him a high five on the new packaging. She wanted to be reminded what it felt like to see real people take these actions or possibly even take them herself without inwardly researching the emotional response of onlookers in order to determine whether or not they would buy pens who were affectionate in that particular way. She looked across the table at Sonja, a woman in her mid-fifties who had been with the company thirty years. She noticed Sonja's skin was the same color as the bland, taupe paint on the office walls and wondered if this would eventually happen to her, if it perhaps was already happening to her, if her life would also be absorbed into this place where she spent most of her time. She suddenly understood that Fountain Friends really didn't have any relation to her life, except for the fact that it was her life.

She again tried to stand up, but this time her skirt got caught on the underbelly of the chair, so she sat back down. "You're right. My life has nothing to do with this ad," she said and suddenly wondered what life was like in other places, beyond the conference room with its familiar surroundings, beyond the well worn path from work to home to the grocery store to the gas station and back to work again. She hadn't even left the city limits in two years. She looked at the dark pools under Sonja's eyes and pictured Sonja in Jamaica, serving rum drinks and jerk chicken at a street café, and in this vision the darkness disappeared, perhaps flowed into the ocean and evaporated in the sunshine-filled world around her. She pictured herself somewhere else too, somewhere inspired where walls were painted lush colors and she could see without squinting under florescent lights.

"Okay. Well, then let's get back to it," Tom said.

She was trapped, but she didn't know why. It would be so easy to just get up and leave, clothing constraints aside, but where would she go after she left the room? Tom looked at her as if to say, *Pay attention, young lady. Your success here is dependent on your actions in meetings like this one.* But Tom had no real authority over her life, so why had she let him control most of her movements and even her thoughts for the past eight years?

Tom talked about the percentage of sales increase the company could expect if the pens were moved up one shelf and were closer to a customer's eye level, and Holly picked at the run in her nylons and tried to remember a time when she felt true passion. The day she was offered the job, her mother and father took her out for a steak dinner and toasted the beginning of a prosperous future, but was that true passion? She had had boyfriends and let them have sex with her, but she often caught herself daydreaming about tasks she had to complete at work the next day. Once in a while she indulged in a long bath, put her hair in a tight bun, submerged her hair in the water, and felt the air bubbles snake their way through her scalp. The tingling sensation lasted a few minutes before the air pockets were all filled in with water, but those few minutes were pure pleasure. She suddenly had an intense desire to go home and take a bath. She could claim sickness, food poisoning from the new restaurant on 7th Street, but her allegiance to the company was too strong.

She watched as James, the summer intern, pretended to be shopping for pens in order to demonstrate to the group how integral placement of the product really was. "See," Tom said. "It's highly unlikely that the customer will reach or stoop just to purchase a pen. We aren't selling kitty litter. Low weight items are expected to be low resistance pick ups."

Her first year with the company, she never listened to the radio in the car. Instead she spoke aloud to herself, practicing points she would bring up in meetings. After missing the turn onto her street a couple of times, she started listening to the radio again, deciding that music was more conducive to active driving. Tom once called the office a "music free zone," stating that music stirs up emotions in its listeners, and those emotions can stifle the ability to be productive.

"So we want to cater to lazy people?" Holly asked.

"We want to cater to the majority of the population, and the majority of the population wants shopping to be an easy thing. They will, in fact, pay more for an item just because it is easily accessible to them."

"So I'm going to spend the next two months of my life calling all the stores in the state and begging them to move our pens up one shelf?"

"Not exactly," Tom said. "Some of the stores in the northeast portion of the state have been stocking us high, so you would want to convince them to move us down. I have the whole chart printed out in my office. We're going to devote July and August to our 'Move to the Middle' campaign."

She had done this before, several times, only to have the product moved back a few months later. To her it felt like buying a house, owning it for a year, and finding out that it was no longer hers and had to be repurchased. She could never truly make progress, and even if she did, she was still afraid to walk by the office supplies aisle in the store by her condo, always fearing that the pens would be moved from their agreed-upon position.

"I remember. We did this last January, and now the stores have shifted their shelf position again," she said.

"Yes. That's expected. It's all part of the retail game. I feel very optimistic about this, though. The fact that we are being stocked high in some stores, which, I might add, has never happened before, tells me that things are going well."

"Do you ever wonder how many hours in your day you are a slave, how few moments you feel completely alive and content in your reality?" Holly asked and noticed the nervous glances on the faces of the others in that little room.

"Holly, I think you may be running a fever. It's almost three. Why don't you take the last two hours as vacation and go home and get some rest? We're going to need you at full capacity the rest of the week," he said.

She thought about what it would be like to drive home without traffic and watch a late afternoon talk show while eating cheese and crackers like a kid after school. She knew she would be back tomorrow, probably before eight, to make phone calls all day to annoyed store managers, begging them to move a few packages of pens to a different location, but she kept thinking about that sentence, the one she had almost underlined even though it was a library book, the one about passion and optimistically predicting one's future. "You're probably right. I've been feeling a little off today," she said. "Thanks for understanding." She picked up her pen and folder and went back to her desk to gather her purse and sunglasses. She rode the elevator alone and walked quickly to her car as Tom and the others watched her from the conference room window. Driving home, she clicked the radio volume knob up two notches, and it felt like she was floating as her car flew down empty streets and sailed smoothly into an unfilled parking lot.

Emergency Repairman

"What seems to be the problem?" I asked after poking my head into the white office and staring seriously at the man wearing the argyle sweater and black pants.

"The machine is malfunctioning again," he said and handed me a clipboard.

"Is it the rotator blades or the engine?" I asked.

"That, I am unable to say. I'm just glad you arrived so quickly, man. Things are beginning to unravel down there."

"Yes. Yes. I know," I said and began to fill out the document with my name, company, and other pertinent information.

"The urgency is sensed down there. Try to calm the workers when you begin. We all need a little easing," he said to me and scratched at the bald spot on his head.

"I understand this better than you think," I said. "Remember I do this all day, every day. They will surely realize I'm a professional," and I pointed to the badge on the side of my red polo shirt as he gave me an unsteady smile and proceeded to explain.

"I first got the call about an hour ago. I sensed a nervousness in that young man's voice as I attempted to assure him that it was certainly not his fault."

"Placing blame is a common reaction," I said and continued, "It's worse when it's yourself that you blame. Guilt usually comes into play."

"It does and even more so with the new workers. The older ones realize adjustments must be made occasionally, but the new ones are just so unprepared."

"It perhaps should be our job, in part, to prepare them," I said.

"The problem is that one never really does know how one will react in such a situation," he said.

"Yes, how to face the hordes of people and relay that message, that horrific news, is practically un-teachable." I noticed his slumped shoulders, his eyes that seemed dead to the world, and understood his position and the need he possessed for my trained body and mind. "We will make this right," I said.

"Yes, we must," he said, and he fell into a nearby chair to wait anxiously for my return with news to ease him.

I left that office with a determination unique to my occupation. Failing was not an option. I woke every morning to the feeling of my heart beating slightly faster than it should and repeated to myself, "I change lives. I alter the problem many cannot, and, though often times it becomes stressful, I know how important I am." These self talks usually woke my wife and provoked phrases like, "I'm trying to sleep;" "You worry too much," and, perhaps the worst, "This obsession is going to end us." I knew it could, but a president would choose his job over marriage, a heart surgeon, and, of course, I would as well.

The layout of the building slowed me with its winding hallways and long corridors. I pressed the elevator button and waited for a few moments before deciding the stairs were better, that I could carry myself down faster than the elevator if I made coordination take first place in my mind.

Just past the halfway point of bounding down the steps, I saw a young woman with long brown hair pulled back into a braid and a mouth that looked lost without the smile that I inferred was usually there. "You're here. Thank God," she said. "A state of panic is beginning to form down there. I had to get out. I don't know how much longer the others are going to last." She gulped in huge amounts of air and shook her head in disbelief.

"It's okay. It's okay," I said and held up my toolbox.

"Have you ever . . ." She looked down at my black work boots and softly kicked her leg with her tennis shoe.

"Ever what?" I asked, trying not to show my own concern for the situation by standing tall and making my voice lower than its natural range.

"Have you ever failed to recover a . . ."

"No," I said, cutting her short. "No. I am perfectly accurate. Don't worry about that."

"I'm just afraid that . . ." she started.

"Don't be," I said. "Don't be afraid," I repeated and felt my whole body shake, trying so intensely to convince her and forget my own doubts, my own distrust in my abilities.

"Good luck," she said.

"I don't need luck," I replied and bounded down the remainder of the steps as she slowly crept upward.

I walked the rest of the way to the sight so as not to alarm the workers. They stood there in a cloud of disorientation as though they had been asked to speak a new language. I broke through the threshold and announced, "I'm a professional. There's no need to tear yourselves apart or search for the impossible words to tell them anymore. I will reverse all the damage immediately."

I worked quickly and efficiently, pulling dented rotator blades out and replacing them with fresh ones that could restore the original process. I wiped down every surface of the machine and watched my hands work with the same exhilarated feeling a baseball player must experience as he saves the team from the mistakes of the other players.

When I was finished, I turned to the workers and announced, "Everything is in working order again. The machine is fully functional." No one clapped for me, but I could feel their breathing return to a relaxed state, and I knew the days ahead were better for both the workers and customers because of my services.

The job of the slushy repairman is tedious and often goes unappreciated, but that day I lingered at the job site for a while and took particular notice of the masses carrying strawberry, chocolate banana, and blue raspberry slushies. I watched strangers taking sips of pleasure, sips that only existed because of my presence. The workers fell back into the safety of routine, no longer having to suggest a Coke instead and deliver the horrible news of the malfunctioning machine. Surely the greatest minds of earth realize that soda could never replace the amazing goodness of flavored ice shavings traveling to that place deep within.

An Unpacked Suitcase

We sat behind the front window of her house looking out at the absence of activity that always occupied the empty road. Her house was on Willow Street, which ran parallel to five other streets with names of trees—Elm, Birch, Pine, Spruce, and Cedar. The simplicity was sickening.

Rose had me over to her house every Thursday evening for what she called "time away." She made her husband, Steve, take the kids somewhere so she and I could experience an hour of freedom from the life she had chosen. Sometimes I didn't want to go, but I always did. Rose was assigned to be my prayer partner when I joined the Methodist church in town four years ago, but after a few meetings, our relationship developed into more than the one year obligation she agreed to and grew into a friendship.

"Rose, I'm gonna move. I'm serious this time. There's nothing for me here anymore, and I'm starting to wonder if there ever was. I have to get out of this town and my life here. I'm bored all the time now," I said.

"Daphne, I've heard this all before. You know this is where you belong. Your life is here."

"But it doesn't have to be," I said and stared at the vacant street.

"Have some pie," she said.

"No. Pie isn't going to fix anything. What I need to do is go home, find my suitcase, start packing, and just pick a place and move."

"You're probably just having a bad week. You said it yourself: the diner has been crazy lately."

"No, it's not that. I'm not happy here."

"Just relax and have some pie," she said. I watched the breeze push leaves down the street outside her window and tried to remember what color my suitcase was. "It's banana cream," she said.

* * *

For three years I have blamed my position in life on Rose's pie. I probably should have stopped bringing up the conversation, but it seemed like if I didn't verbalize my dissatisfaction with life then I would really be stuck forever. Somehow I had almost started to accept the routine of discontent and had even begun to ignore the fresh concept of starting something new.

"Daph, you'll be late for work if you lie in bed anymore." I told Jim when we started dating not to call me Daph, but he kept forgetting.

"I showered last night. I'm fine," I said and watched Jim grab the night stand and roll his body off the side of the bed, a technique he had developed in order to avoid the pain of sitting up straight to get out of bed. Since we started dating, he had put on so much weight that even black colored shirts could no longer help him. I watched him saunter sleepily to the bathroom and listened to the soothing sound of the shower. I started counting the red flowers on the wallpaper, but I never got beyond the first strip before the water stopped. I would have liked him to stay in there all day.

"What are your hours today?" he screamed from the bathroom.

"Eight to six," I yelled back.

"Better get up then. I thought you worked early today." He appeared with a brown towel wrapped around his neck, and I wondered how many weeks it had been since we had sex.

"It's only 7:15. It takes me three minutes to drive to work and only ten minutes to get ready, which means I have to get out of bed at a quarter to eight. You know this," I said.

"Fine, but don't be mad at me when you're late someday." He threw his towel on his side of the bed, and I threw it on the floor and turned away to try to get back to my thirty minutes of sleep.

* * *

I worked at Duncan's Diner as a waitress and hated every moment there slightly more than the last. Every day the same twenty people came in and ordered the same menu items they had every day since I moved to Mainard. My mother had always preached "more opportunities in Mainard" because it's bigger than Crawford, which is where I grew up. I listened and moved the eighteen miles to a town of 1,806 people and away from Crawford's measly population of 386. Mother seemed to think it was a great accomplishment. I knew better. After nearly five years in Mainard, the colors were draining out of my life there, and all I could see was brown—Jim's brown work pants, the brown bedspread we slept under and experienced bitter dreams beneath, the brown carpet that came with my apartment, the brown booths at the diner, and the brown eyes that never seemed to notice me anymore.

I met Jim at the street dance in town the summer I moved in. I remember that he commented on my shirt, a black tank top with strawberries on the straps, and, for some reason, this was all it took. He moved in three weeks later, and we shared my one bedroom apartment blissfully happy for about a month and a half before his annoying habits started to create my misery. He was one of those nondescript-looking people, a guy that I knew would easily fade into the dark hallways of memory shortly after our break-up. His dull eyes, thinning hair, and muted features made him look older than twenty-nine. I always knew that I would eventually ask him to leave, but somehow I just hadn't gotten around to it yet.

* * *

"Daph, did you wash my shirts with your whites?" Jim asked.

"No. Did you want me to?"

"Oh, come on!" he said. "I asked you at least twice this morning."

"I was probably asleep."

"You sleep a lot," he said.

"There's not much to be awake for."

"Why do you have to talk like that, Daph? When was the last time we went out and did something fun? You just want to sit around at night and do nothing."

"Can't you see that I'm trying to read?" I asked and held up the book about Arctic expeditions that was so worn that some of the pages had detached from the binding.

"Just make sure you wash them tonight," he said and left the room.

* * *

While watching Jim wash dishes that night, I suddenly remembered the last time we had sex. It was four and a half months before, the night he took me to dinner in a town called Sherman, a thirteen mile drive west through the stark prairie of Oklahoma. We ate pepperoni pizza at The Pizza Palace. He had said, "Daph, you look so good," and I felt like he could see me again.

We ate the rest of the meal like we always did, silently with only an occasional break for some tedious small talk, but I kept thinking about the compliment, and, as I drank more beer, it seemed better and better. On the way from Sherman, the blankness of the dark prairie sky and the comfort of the car and the absence of deer running across the road made me momentarily happy again. When we got home that night, I threw a load of laundry into the dryer. The rhythmic sound filled the apartment and overpowered the soft moans of our mediocre sex.

"I'm bored," I said as he folded a dish towel and hung it on the rack.

"You're bored?"

"Yeah."

"Come to Zach's game with me tomorrow."

"I don't think that will help," I said and pulled my short blonde hair into a ponytail.

"What are you bored of? Is it because it's almost summer, and all your shows are gonna be reruns?"

"No. This has got nothing to do with TV. I'm just bored. I've been bored. I'm tired all the time lately. Haven't you noticed? Every day is the same damn thing. I get up, go to work, come home. It's always an exact copy of the day before. Sometimes I think I would be saved from all of this if Merle just ordered a different kind of pie."

"Okay . . ."

"I mean, don't these people understand that usual doesn't mean always? If they never plan on ordering anything different then they should just be honest about it. If they're going to stick to the same obsessive patterns they have had for years and years then why not just say, 'I'll have the always.' 'Give me the always'? Why do they say, 'Give me the usual'?"

"Maybe you need a few days off," he said.

"Why? What's the point? Unless these people all die during my three days off or realize the concept of eating at home it's not going to make any difference. I was bored with this job after two days of working there. Things aren't going to somehow get better," I said.

"Life is boring, Daph. That's just the way it is," he said.

"And you're okay with that?" I asked.

"You just have to find something interesting within the boredom," he said, and I thought back to a few weeks ago when Douglas, one of my regulars, had accidentally worn one brown and one black sock. "I'm going to bed," he said.

I sat up late that night watching an infomercial for a mop that could absorb all the water in a swimming pool, and I wished for that kind of magic in my life.

* * *

The next Sunday I decided to walk home from church. It was a perfect late April day, so I told Rose to go on without me. She usually gave me a ride to the hardware store where Jim worked, and he drove me home during his fifteen minute break at noon. His store was the only business in town open on Sundays, and in a town as small as Mainard, people used the hardware store as a social gathering more than a place to buy nails and paint. Jim enjoyed the short drive and the few minutes at home because he disliked the hectic atmosphere of the store on Sundays.

"Are you sure you don't want a ride?" Rose yelled from the open window of her maroon station wagon while Steve sat in the driver seat looking anxious to get home.

"I'm sure. Thanks, though."

"Jim is going to wonder where you are," she said.

"Let him wonder," I said and started walking the mile home.

I noticed the subdued green leaves on the trees that lined the street and wondered how different the trees looked in other parts of the world. Of course I had seen pictures of palm trees and vast forests in books, but I wanted to touch the trunks and see the soil that nourished them. I had never really been anywhere. My father worked as a bus driver for the rural school systems, and my mother stayed home to raise my three sisters and me, so the money supply was tight. We took a few short trips to Tulsa to visit my aunt and uncle, but I had never left Oklahoma.

That afternoon walk, though merely a slight deviation from my normal Sunday routine, was somehow empowering. It wasn't like I was required to ride with Jim and engage in ten minutes of dull conversation, but I had begun to believe it was required.

Stepping outside of the schedule felt good, but, as I came into view of my apartment, I saw Jim standing outside. I thought about turning down a side street and hiding until he had to go back to work, but I kept on walking, and he started jogging toward me. Out of breath and clearly annoyed, he said, "Rose said you decided to walk today."

"Yeah, I did."

"Why?"

"Because it's a nice day out, and I wanted a change."

"It's been nice out before, and you still let me drive you home," he said and squinted as the sun emerged from its position behind a cloud.

"Well, today I felt like walking."

"Fine, I guess I can take an extra fifteen minutes so we can talk," he said, and I realized I hadn't really changed anything.

We proceeded to have the same conversation we always had on Sunday afternoons. He told me about the unrealistic demands of his boss and the irritating ignorance of his customers, and I pretended to listen.

* * *

"Rose, I hate him. I'm living with a man that I hate, and I hate myself for doing it," I said and took another bite of her delicious lemon bar.

"He's perfectly nice to you," she said. "I don't understand what you're complaining about."

"He's just so boring. He has no aspirations to do anything outside of someday taking over the hardware store. We haven't had a real conversation in years," I said.

"You don't hate him. You're just going through what my mother called relationship anxiety. It's completely normal and doesn't last forever."

I wondered how long her relationship anxiety had been going on.

"What would I be anxious about?" I asked.

"I think you might be a little afraid of marriage," she said.

"Marriage? I have no intention of marrying Jim. I only let him move in because things were going well at the time, and the rent is lower with him paying half, but now it's gotten all out of control, and I don't know how to stop it."

"Daphne, you shouldn't be living in sin if you never intend to get out of it by marrying Jim."

"We can't even have a conversation, so how could I possibly marry him?"

"That's just how men are. No one talks to their spouse much after they get married. Steve and I just do our own thing. That's the problem with dating for years. That's not the way it's supposed to work or no one would get married. Men have about six months of conversational capacity in them, and then they dry up forever. Jim should have proposed to you during that first year."

"That's a horrible system."

"It's not. You get used to it, and once you have kids, they keep you busy anyway." I didn't feel like questioning her anymore, so I slumped back into the couch and spent the last thirty minutes there listening to her brag about her daughter, Megan's, unusually large vocabulary for a six-year-old.

* * *

"Jeb, is that cheeseburger almost up for table four?" I asked the cook while making salads for Jess and Sandy at table one.

"Two minutes, babe."

"Okay."

Four o'clock was always busy with people in for supper. Since over half the town consisted of retired people, they made their visit to the diner for supper a daily ritual, and every day I watched them amble in and sit with the same people at the same table. On the rare occasion that people from out of town passed through and decided to stop at the diner, the locals acted as though the out-of-towners had come into their very own homes uninvited and sat down at their personal tables expecting to be fed. They couldn't fully grasp the concept that they did not own or even reserve their table. I, on the other hand, happily welcomed these strange faces because they almost always tipped more.

"Ginnie, the pink tulips in your yard are just wonderful," I said while pouring her coffee.

"Yes, they came a little later this year than last. I think it's a good sign. Maybe we won't have such a hot summer."

I smiled and turned to Dorothy, "Would you like some more coffee too?"

"Are you trying to kill me, dear? I couldn't have any more. I'm already on my fifth cup." Ginnie smiled at me apologetically. The day before, Dorothy had yelled at me for not filling her cup up when it was almost empty.

"Number three up," I heard Jeb yell from the kitchen. I rushed to the back and picked up a plate to bring to Sam, a man in his eighties who always came alone.

"You know it's rough when all your friends have passed away and your wife died years ago," he said.

"I know, Sam," I said and handed him the liver and onions with a side of creamed corn.

"No, you're too young to understand that, but wait until you get to be my age. Then you'll know what it's like." Sam told me this every day.

"Would you like another glass of orange juice?"

"You know, I never liked orange juice until I married Esther. It was always her favorite, and even when she got older she always had this child-like smile on her face when she drank orange juice. Now I drink it all the time." I nodded and headed to the kitchen to get him a second glass.

* * *

I went home after work to find Jim asleep on the couch with the television blasting information about the addictive qualities of bowling. I reached for the remote that was lying on Jim's bare stomach, and he suddenly flapped his arms madly while shouting, "What the fuck? What the fuck?"

"Jim, wake up. It's just me."

"Daph, you scared the shit out of me."

"How was work?" I asked.

"Good." He never asked about my day. Instead he said, "I haven't eaten yet."

"Me either," I said.

"Could you maybe offer to make something, Daph? I'm starving."

"Why don't you cook tonight? I'm pretty hungry myself and worked more hours than you today," I said.

"Never mind," he said. "I'll just grab a bag of chips." I watched him shuffle pathetically into the kitchen and waited for him to return with the chips.

He didn't, so I followed him into the kitchen. "You're eating in here?" I asked.

"Yep."

"Why?"

"You're obviously in a bad mood today, so I thought I'd do us both a favor and give you some space," he said and shoved another handful of broken sour cream and onion chips into his mouth.

"Do *us* both a favor? Doing me a favor would be to have dinner ready for me when I get home. It isn't easy to watch people eat all night, you know, to have to see them enjoying the food I serve but not being able to sit down and eat too. It's not like I expect you to help me out on a regular basis, which is a good thing considering the fact that it's never happened, but every once in a while maybe you could stop being so selfish and think about me, about what would make me happy."

"Okay . . . so do you want some chips?"

* * *

"Well, I think that's progress," Rose said as the sound of her husband's car disappeared down the block.

"He asked me to share the chips I bought."

"He's a man."

"That doesn't give him a ticket to be completely unaware of my desires at all times."

"So just ask him to take you out. Men can't figure things out on their own. They need to be guided."

"I can't believe that that's true of all men. There must be some men who actually think about what women want."

"Just tell him," she said.

"But that defeats the whole purpose."

"What purpose?"

"Part of the appeal of a guy taking a woman out is the fact that he's doing it from his own desire to make her happy."

"Where does this actually happen? Do you mean that you don't only expect Jim to take you out but you expect it to be his idea as well? Men don't have ideas. They can't plan things. It's a well known fact."

"Why?"

"Because they don't think about things the way women do."

"I think we just know the wrong men," I said and realized I was annoying Rose.

"Let's talk about something else, okay?" she said.

"Good idea," I said and took a sip of iced tea.

That night, as we discussed possible wallpaper patterns for Rose's bathroom, I realized that she was trapped in her house and in her life. The wedding picture of Rose and Steve stood in its frame on the end-table and served as a reminder of what could happen to me if I wasn't very careful. I could almost see my own future house with a wedding picture and other artifacts of a life I didn't want. Rose's living room was an assortment of her life as a couple—posed pictures of her children, a shelf of miniature tea sets her mother-in-law gave her for birthday presents, the ugly floral vase Steve bought her for an anniversary present, and animal figurines she bought him to compensate for his unlived dream of a career in wildlife photography. I was afraid. I knew I had to get out somehow, but I didn't know which door to use or which direction to walk once I passed through.

The Chess Master

I

It's seven p.m. at Bayou City Café, and he sits waiting. I often wonder how long he's been coming here and what brought him in that first time with a suitcase of chess sets and a clipboard to record wins and losses. I sit alone at a table in the corner, clacking away on my computer, writing a test for my American Literature class, and he ambles over, places his cracked hands on my table and says, "Care for a game of chess, Dina?"

I answer, "No, thanks. I have a lot of work to do." He shakes his head in disgust and walks away.

I've never played chess with Lyle Weatherford, but he keeps asking. In fact, he has asked every time he's seen me for the past six years.

II

"Pardon me. I hope I'm not interrupting. It's nice seeing you again, Sandra," Lyle says and grabs Mindy's hand.

"This isn't Sandra. This is Mindy," I reply, trying desperately to downplay a potentially awkward situation.

"Where is Sandra?" he asks. "I liked playing chess with her."

"I'm not sure," I reply. "Lyle, I'm actually on a date right now, so maybe Sam would be interested in playing you."

"Nope, no such luck. I already asked him. He has some deadline for work or something like that. Anyway, Sandra always played with such aggression. She was a real killer. Why don't you just call her and get her down here? That will solve everything," he says.

137

I notice Mindy is shifting uneasily in her chair, and her eyes seem to search the room for an exit. "Look, Lyle. I don't talk to Sandra anymore," I say.

"What happened?" he asks with an intense level of emotion in his voice, more emotion than I felt the night Sandra ended our six month relationship.

"We broke up," I say and look awkwardly at my date.

"You broke up with Sandra for this girl? Sandra was much prettier than this girl, and she could play chess."

"Please go play chess with someone else. I'm on a date, and it was going pretty well until you came over here."

"Do you have Sandra's number?" he asks.

"No."

"How can you have dated someone for so long and not have her number?" he asks.

"I deleted it when I met this beautiful woman," I say and hope for a smile from Mindy but only get a look of annoyance.

"Well, what's her last name? We'll look her up. That'll solve it." His face lights up again as he must be remembering the night Sandra patiently played six games with him as I hurried to finish grading my stack of eighth grade history exams.

"Don't you understand that it might be awkward for my ex-girlfriend to be here when I'm on a date? Doesn't it register with you that I don't want to see Sandra anymore, that she's out of my life now?" I know it doesn't, and the quizzical look on his face as he leans in closer confirms this.

"Why doesn't anyone want to play chess anymore?" he mumbles and repeats louder, "Why doesn't anyone want to play chess anymore?"

"People have other things going on," I say. "People don't always want to play chess. Sometimes they want to have a conversation or get work done or enjoy meeting someone new."

"There is nothing better than chess," he says and walks away. I watch him approach a group of high school kids at a table across the way, and I turn to an exhausted looking Mindy.

"Did you just get out of a relationship, John?" she asks me. "Is this a rebound date?"

I suddenly realize that Lyle is playing chess all the time, and that tonight, in the chess-like conversation that just took place between Lyle and me, Lyle won.

III

Lyle Weatherford is one of my regulars. During orientation three years ago, a co-worker filled me in on the must-have information about this guy. "He comes in every night, kind of harasses the customers, tries to set his chess boards on all the back tables, and dresses real weird, but he buys a lot of stuff, so Kevin encourages him."

"Gotcha," I said, and I scanned the room for Lyle. "Is he here now?"

"Nah, his schedule changes, but he's always here by ten," he said.

I left work at six that first night, but it didn't take long for me to become acquainted with Lyle. I've been working at Bayou City Café for a little over a year now, and I often catch myself watching Lyle as I make sandwiches or wipe down the tables in the dining room. Tonight he is wearing a shirt that says *Chess Is Life* across the front in big black letters. In the past year I have noticed that he sports a variety of chess t-shirts: *Got Chess?*; *Check Mate*; *It's a Knight, not a Horse!*; *I'd rather be playing chess*; *Life is a game. Chess is serious.*; and *Wanted: Chess Players*. On the rare occasions that he is not wearing a chess-themed shirt, he puts on a button that says *Peace, Love, and Chess*. He always wears cotton shorts or sweat pants, a sweat band on his head, and white tennis shoes. He puts his watch on over a red wrist band, and he always attaches a yellow retainer rope to his large glasses (although I've never seen him take them off). His thin white hair is combed straight back, his legs and arms are scrawny and mostly hairless, but his mid-section is solid, and his hands are large and strong looking.

Lyle is seventy-one but still works full-time as a radio station manager, and I can't understand how he stays out so late every night, sometimes past one a.m., sometimes even past three. It's a little before midnight, and he appears to be finishing up a game with David, a college guy who plays a few games with Lyle almost every week. A customer approaches me. She looks

139

like a college student, probably stressed out because finals start next week. Her hair is haphazardly pulled back into a messy bun, and her grey sweat pants have noticeable food stains in several places. "What can I get you?" I ask.

"I hate to bother you with this, but could you possibly get that man to move some of his chess boards? They're taking up several tables in the back room, and I need a place to sit."

"No one's sitting there?" I ask.

"Nope, it's just the boards."

"Okay, I'll take care of it. Sorry about that."

"Thanks," she says, and I feel my stomach drop a little. I have never had a run-in with Lyle before, but I've heard stories, and those stories usually don't end well.

I finish making a hot cocoa, wash my hands, and head out to the lobby to confront Lyle. He's busy studying the clipboard and making notes about his last game. "Excuse me," I say. He doesn't hear me, probably because he always has cotton balls shoved into his ears for a reason unknown to me. "Excuse me," I say again, but this time loud enough for him to hear.

He looks up. "Care for a game of chess, Karen? Is your shift all done?"

"No, I'm actually on for another two hours. I was just wondering if you could possibly move some of your boards. There are customers who need a place to sit."

"I would like to, but I'm sure you see my dilemma. The problem is that I've done that before, the last time being March fifth, and then comes a flurry of players, and I can't accommodate them. You see the problem, right?"

"I do, but we have to do things on a first-come, first-served basis here, and I have customers who need tables now."

"Well, if it's first-come, first-served then I came first. I was here before these other people, and I claimed my tables."

"I understand that, but since no one is at the tables, I'm going to need you to move your boards."

I can tell he's getting flustered. He looks at the table and taps the eraser end of the pencil against the side of his face. "I can't do that. I can't do that. If they come, I won't be prepared. I know you're worried about customers and such because this is your business, but this is my business. I have to worry about my people too."

His business? I don't know how to reason with Lyle. This was definitely not covered in my week of training. "I don't have a choice. If you don't move the boards, I'll get into trouble. I'll get fired."

"Just let me talk to Kevin. He'll straighten everything out," he says.

"Kevin is off today. I don't know what else to tell you. You need to move the boards. Kevin would say the same thing."

"I'll call him up. Do you have his home number?"

"No, he doesn't give us that information."

"Then I guess we're at an impasse," he says and shrugs his shoulders.

When I applied for the job at Bayou City Café, I thought the hard part would be learning how to make the various coffee drinks. I was wrong. I don't know what else to say to Lyle. His position appears fixed, and I can tell that I am losing. A guy I used to date played chess sometimes, and when he felt like winning was impossible, he tipped his king over and nodded in defeat to his opponent. "So you're not going to move the boards? There's nothing I can say to convince you?"

"No, I don't think so. Only Kevin could talk me into doing that. I just can't do that to my people," he says.

"Well, if you change your mind, I would really appreciate it," I say and walk away. The girl who requested a table is standing in front of the counter when I get there. I shrug my shoulders and say, "He refuses to move. There's nothing we can do."

IV

I have two loves in my life: chess and coffee. I don't think my wife ever really understood that. I told her on our first date, but, as the years passed, it always seemed like she didn't believe me. Harriet and I were married the first time for six years. She started complaining about my chess time a few months in, and the complaints only intensified the further we got along.

"Why were you out until three a.m.?" "Why didn't you at least call?" "Why are all our vacations for your chess tournaments where I am forced to entertain myself in the hotel or in some strange city while you play chess all day?" "Why do you spend all your time at home reading strategy books?" "Why don't you want to have children with me?" "Why are you always at that coffee shop?" "Why?" "Why?" "Why?" On and on she goes.

After six years, we still couldn't manage to settle in to each others' ideals, so we divorced.

The two years apart were the best years of my life. I stayed at Bayou City Café all night seven nights a week and played chess with what seemed like everyone in town. Teachers, lawyers, pharmacists, waiters, salesmen, retired folks, and young children were all eager to learn a game that could soothe the end of their life or start them on the right path. Black, white, and Asian folks, women and men, American and foreign, rich and poor, all the customers of that coffee shop came to play with me. Hell, I even played chess with the mayor one fateful evening, and I beat him. It was a thrill to know that in the game everything else in the world fell away, and it was a comfort not having to worry about an angry woman just sitting up all night waiting to yell at me when I walked through the door.

But after that carefree retreat, Harriet started coming around again. I guess the two years apart made her realize that I wasn't such a bad guy after all. She brought me pies and sometimes even a casserole. Her brother called me frequently, saying I should remarry her, that we had made a mistake and given up too quickly before. He said that life is long and two years apart didn't have to ruin a lifetime of love. I liked the pie, and Harriet doing my wash was so much more convenient than taking it to the laundry service once a week, so, on an unbearably hot August day, Harriet and I went to the courthouse and got married again.

Before our second marriage, she once said, "I don't know what I was so upset about. It's not like you were having an affair. You just really like chess."

"No, I love chess," I said and looked at the framed picture of a check mate above Harriet's head.

"I know," she said and shook her head, but she was smiling.

It didn't take long after our second wedding for that smile to disappear, but she didn't complain as much the second time around, and I was happy to have found a good balance in life. I had chess, and I had someone to ride with me when I took long car rides to visit old chess rivals.

I didn't have to cook anymore, and the house smelled better with Harriet's soaps and lotions in it.

The other night Harriet was getting ready for bed after a long bath. The weather was stormy, and there were tornado warnings, so none of my usual opponents were at the café, and I came home early. I was in bed with my laptop, playing chess with a guy from Indiana. "Lyle?" she said.

"Just a sec. I'm about to wrap this one up," I said and studied the screen.

"You've been on that all night. Can't we talk a little?"

"Yes, yes, of course. Just a sec."

"Damn it. Am I invisible?" she shouted, and she rushed over to the outlet and unplugged the computer.

"I have battery backup, Harriet. You know that. Just give me a second," I said. I knew I could beat the guy even though he was rated a little higher than me.

"Damn it!" she shouted again and ran out of the room. I was relieved to have time to finish out the game. It would have been awful to waste an hour and not experience the climax.

It all came down to his queen and my knight and bishop, but, in the end, he was a better player than me. He slowly drove me into a corner, and there was nothing I could do. I thought about going downstairs to see if Harriet was baking something but decided instead to start another game. Maybe I could beat this guy after all, I thought.

The game was just getting interesting when I noticed Harriet standing in the doorway. "You're still playing that game?" she asked.

"Well, technically this is a different game. I lost the last one, and it was really close. I figured I better . . ."

"You what? You started another game?" she shouted.

"This guy is a real killer. It's hard to find players like this locally. There was Jack Poppe a few years ago, but he moved on to Chicago. Such a shame! I loved playing with that guy. He was . . ."

"It's like I'm not even here. I should have known this would happen again. I was so stupid." I pushed a pawn and waited for Indiana guy's move. "You're playing another game! Another game!"

"Why don't you put some cookies in the oven, and I'll be down shortly," I said, hoping it would get her out of the room.

"No! We're not doing that again. I'm your wife, and I want to talk to you," she shouted and lunged at me. She grabbed the computer off my lap and ran out into the hall. I heard the crash and ran after her.

I looked over the railing, and there it was. My new computer had been thrown overboard and was resting on the tile floor below. I would never know the outcome of that game. I wondered how this would affect the online rating system.

Harriet was crying. "I shouldn't have done that. I know. But I just couldn't stand it anymore."

"Okay," I said and walked back to the bedroom. She followed me.

"Do you know what the best moment of my life was?" she asked. I looked at the bookshelf and pulled out a strategy book to look up a question I had about the Sicilian Defense. "Do you?" she asked again. I didn't really understand the question. I couldn't read minds, so how would I know?

"No," I said.

"It was that day we went to Galveston when we were first dating. Remember that street café with the huge pina coladas?"

"Kind of."

"We had so much fun that day, and you told me you loved me for the first time." I couldn't find the pages about the Sicilian Defense as quickly as I thought I would, so I flipped to the index. "Remember?" she said.

"Of course. We went to see the huge chess set downtown," I said.

"Yeah, and to enjoy the weather. It was May, I believe. Yes, it was May. I remember because it was right after I went to Boston to see Mom for Mother's Day. Yep, that was my favorite memory. I was falling in love, the sun was shining, and you were so handsome," she said.

"Found it," I said, and my eyes went right to the place I had underlined before, right at the bottom of the page next to the graphs.

"Are you listening?" she said.

"Yeah, that was your favorite day," I said.

"What was yours?" she asked.

I closed the book and put it down. "That's easy," I said.

"Okay . . ."

"The best night of my life was down at the café. A few years back, when we were separated, I played simultaneous chess with ten people at once. They were all lined up, and I raced from table to table, making my move as the others studied their boards and waited for me. We played until four in the morning, but I felt like I could've played forever. I must've had a dozen cups of coffee that night. The best part was that the other customers, the ones who weren't playing, started to take an interest in what was going on. They started watching me. I played and played without mistakes, and believe me—there were some real killers there that night. I finished game after game and never lost. I was like a machine. One guy even said it felt like playing against the computer. Going home that night was horrible. I tried to talk a few of the last players into staying longer, but they said they had to go. I remember knowing, as I drove away from the café, for sure that it would be the best night of my life, and it was. Yep . . . There's no better feeling than that." Harriet started crying and walked out of the room, and I pulled the book back off the shelf and searched again for the section about the Sicilian Defense.

How to Convince a Mother that
Her Son Is Not Her Son

The Question

Is it possible, given the right circumstances, to convince a sane woman that her own child is not her child when she is looking right at him?

The Set-Up

Six months before the experiment, I casually told my mother, during one of our Sunday night phone calls, that a student at the college I was attending looked a lot like my brother, Alan. She chuckled and said, "Really?"

"Yeah," I said. "It's actually a pretty close resemblance. From a distance, the guy is a dead ringer. It kinda freaked me out the first time I saw him."

"That would be fun to see," she said.

I changed the subject and didn't mention the look-alike guy again.

* * *

My parents had plans to visit Texas for a week in March. I was in graduate school and living far from home for the first time. The winters in Minnesota dragged on and on, sometimes well into April, so my parents decided to escape the cold for a few days and spend some time with me in Texas. Alan told them he couldn't come with them because he was playing in a big poker tournament and his band had a gig that weekend. They were disappointed but understood. It was the perfect set-up. All we had to do was orchestrate a situation where Mom and Dad would run into Alan and convince them that it was the look-alike guy. They would rationalize that it couldn't be Alan because he was in Minnesota tending to his planned engagements.

The plan came together one night during a phone conversation with Alan.

"Rick will pick you up at the airport. I'll tell Mom and Dad he's at work," I said to Alan. Rick was my husband and an integral part of the plan.

"Okay, that should work. We'll just kill time somewhere where you guys won't run into us."

"That should be easy. Rick has a lot of friends from work. You could always hang out at one of their places."

"Sure, sure," he said.

"I've been thinking about the location for the run-in, and I think Applebee's is the right place."

"How so?"

"The setup there is perfect. The bar is in the center of the restaurant and is visible from all the tables. You can be sitting up there before we get there. Rick will drop you off. I'll tell Mom and Dad he's getting off work at, say, six and that we're meeting him at Applebee's. Anywhere the waiter seats us will work."

"Okay, I think this is on the right track, but what if Mom and Dad don't feel like Applebee's?"

"They're not usually picky about restaurant choices."

"I know, but I'm trying to play out all the possible scenarios."

"I'll just insist. I'll say that Rick has been craving it or something."

"Okay, that should work. Okay . . . so I'll be sitting up at the bar—"

"Right, and then we'll come in and get seated, settle in, look at the menus for a couple of minutes . . . and then I'll casually look up at the bar and say, 'Hey, that's the guy who looks like Alan.' . . . something like that."

"We're definitely on the right track, but it still seems a little sloppy. I just think they'll know it's me right away."

"But I mentioned months ago that a guy on campus looks like you."

"I know. I know, but I still think they'll know. We need to make it more real. Why would I be sitting at an Applebee's bar at dinner time all alone?"

"It's not you, remember? It's the look-alike guy."

"I know. That's not my point. Why would any college-aged guy be doing that? It doesn't really make sense. Plus, if I'm alone, they'll be more likely to approach me and kill the prank right away." Alan was about to spend money on a plane ticket for a practical joke, and he didn't want it to be for nothing.

"Yeah, I guess that's just a risk we have to take if we decide to do this," I said.

"No, I don't think so. I think I need to be sitting there with someone. That way it seems more natural. I could be on a fake date or something."

"You're right! This is better. I could have Rick get a girl he works with to just sit there with you. We can offer to pay her or something."

"Good. That's what I'm talking about. Also, I probably shouldn't wear my own clothes. That would give me away. I'll borrow clothes from Jordan or something."

"Good idea."

"And I should probably change my hair . . . maybe cut it really short . . . and get a spray tan maybe."

"You're right. You can't look exactly the same or they'll know it's you."

"Exactly!"

We were there. The plan was in place. All that was left was to book a flight for Alan, find a pretend date, and make sure Rick was off work the day of the experiment.

The Delivery

The day of the experiment, my parents and I ate lunch at a café downtown and spent the rest of the afternoon shopping for bargains at the outdoor mall. I looked at my watch far too often and felt my stomach churning with nervous energy. My parents seemed oblivious to my restless nature and commented frequently about the ideal weather conditions.

Meanwhile, Rick drove to Austin to pick Alan up at the airport. They got back to San Marcos around two and spent the rest of the afternoon playing catch and killing time on the grounds of an apartment complex at the edge of town.

Rick dropped Alan off at Applebee's at 5:30 where he met Elise, a twenty-two-year-old who worked with Rick at IHOP. Rick had attempted to explain the experiment to her several times, but she was either too stupid to grasp the concept or had the attention span of a six-year-old with ADD, so he eventually gave up. She had no idea why we wanted her to have dinner with a stranger, but the promise of twenty dollars and a free meal was all the convincing she required. I was nervous she wouldn't show up, but Rick assured me that an IHOP waitress wouldn't pass up an opportunity to make easy money.

At 5:57 we pulled up to the restaurant. Rick was waiting for us in the lobby. The waiter seated us at a booth near the entrance. I walked in front of my parents to strategically seat us so that Mom and Dad's backs were to the bar. Therefore, I could be the one to "discover" him. I quickly glanced up at the bar—we were in perfect position. Alan and Elise were facing our booth but far enough away to be out of earshot and out of close sight range. I opened my menu and pretended to study its contents. "How was work?" Dad asked Rick.

"Good, good. Pretty busy . . . good tips today."

"That's good," Mom said.

"I'm thinking about the quesadillas. What are you guys ordering?" I asked.

"I haven't even looked yet," Mom said and opened her menu.

I wasn't sure how long I should wait before "noticing" them at the bar. I looked back at the menu. "Do you guys have any interest in going to Sea World tomorrow?" Rick asked. "I got some coupons from a customer the other day. He's one of the trainers over there."

"Yeah, that might be fun," I said, knowing that Alan would want to go.

"How far a drive is that?" asked Dad.

"Not too far . . . about an hour," said Rick.

I looked up from my menu, stared straight at Alan for a moment, and said, "Hey—that's the guy who looks like Alan."

"Where?" said Mom.

"Up at the bar," I said and pointed at him.

She turned around and looked up at the bar. "Oh, my God! Oh . . . my . . . God! He looks exactly like him," she almost shouted.

Dad turned around, looked up at the bar, and started to laugh.

"Oh, my God! That's not Alan?" she asked.

"No. Remember? I told you about that guy on campus. He doesn't look as much like him close up, but from a distance it's a pretty good resemblance, right?" I said.

"Pretty good? Pretty good? He looks *exactly* like him. I can't believe that's not him," she said. "Don't you think he looks exactly like Alan?" she asked Rick.

"I don't know. I don't really see it. This guy seems shorter than him or something."

Dad laughed again.

"Don't you think he looks just like him?" she asked Dad.

He looked over his shoulder and said, "Yeah, it's pretty crazy."

"That's not Alan?" she pleaded.

"No. Of course not," I said.

The waiter came over to take our order, but my mom was getting frantic at this point. "Are y'all ready to order?"

"This is going to sound really strange, but there's a guy up at the bar who looks exactly like my son," she said.

The waiter seemed confused. "Do you need another minute to look over the menu?"

"Do you see that guy over there in the blue shirt?" she asked.

The waiter looked over his shoulder and said, "Yeah."

"I'm really confused right now. That's not him?" She looked at me.

"No, it's not him."

"I'll just come back in a few minutes," the waiter said.

"No, it's okay. We're ready," I said and ordered the quesadillas. It was difficult getting Mom to focus long enough to settle on the Oriental chicken salad, but we successfully ordered, and the waiter disappeared.

"Look—he's cracking his knuckles just like Alan does," Dad said. My attention shifted momentarily, and I wondered how awkward the experiment was for Alan, sitting at the Applebee's bar with a girl he had just met, a girl who had such a thick Texas accent that even some of the locals had a hard time understanding her. "I think I'm going to go to the bathroom and wash my hands," he said.

151

"See if you can get a better look at him," Mom pleaded. "Maybe he doesn't look the same up close."

"I don't wanna bother him. He looks like he's on a date." This is what Alan was talking about; this is why Elise was such an integral role to the plan.

"He won't even notice. Just walk past him on your way back," she said.

"Okay," and he was off. We all watched anxiously as he made his way to the bathroom. Mom was hoping that the look-alike was different up close, and I was wondering if Alan could keep his composure with Dad in such close proximity. Dad disappeared into the bathroom for a minute, and then he was back. He took the long way back to the table, walking right behind where Alan and Elise were seated at the bar. I watched as they nonchalantly munched on french fries, and I felt a rush of pride from witnessing the high level of professionalism my brother brought to the experiment. Alan never wavered. His performance was natural and flawlessly believable.

"Well?" Mom asked as Dad sat back down.

"He looks exactly like him."

"Even up close?" she asked.

Dad started to laugh again. "This is really strange," he said.

"Oh, my God! What is happening? I don't understand what is happening," she said. I watched her unraveling in front of me. She had banked on the idea that he looked like a different guy up close. She needed that information in order to make sense of what was happening, but the opposite was true. She didn't know what to do.

"I really don't see it," Rick said. "Alan isn't that tan."

"I'm so confused. How could this be? Do you think . . ." she started.

"What?" I asked.

"You hear those stories about people who have twins and never know it . . ."

"It's probably just a weird coincidence. I'm sure there are a lot of people in the world who look alike. You just never see them."

"Maybe we have relatives we don't know about," she said. "This is the craziest thing I've ever seen!"

"You don't really believe that, do you?" I asked.

"No, it doesn't make any sense, but it also doesn't make any sense that there is a guy in Texas who looks just like him. What is going on? That's really not Alan?"

"No," I said.

"Are you okay?" asked Rick.

"This is the craziest thing! I need to talk to that guy," she said. "I need to see him up close."

"He's on a date. We shouldn't bother him," I said.

"I wish I could take a picture to show Alan. No one is going to believe this," she said.

"You can't just go up to a stranger and take his picture," I said.

"Don, did you bring your camera?" She turned to my dad.

"It's back at the hotel. I didn't think I would need it at Applebee's," he said and laughed.

"I just can't even believe this! What is going on?" she cried.

I wondered how long I should let it go on. Alan and I hadn't discussed the ending much. He just said to give him a nod when I wanted to finish the experiment or when Mom and Dad figured out the truth. I looked up at the bar, and he and Elise were done with their food. When no one was looking, I made eye contact with him and nodded. He called the bartender for the check.

Our waiter came over with the food, and my mother said, "If you saw a guy who looked like your son, would you go and talk to him?"

"I don't have a son," he said.

"But if you did?"

"I don't know. Is there anything else I can bring you right now? Ketchup? Mayo?"

"No, thanks. We're fine," I said, and Alan and Elise were heading our way.

"Oh, my God! They're coming over here," Mom said. "What do I do? What do I do?"

"Just calm down. Don't bother the poor guy," I said.

They were almost to our booth. "I'm sorry," she said to Alan as they passed. "I'm sorry, but I just have to tell you, you look just like my son!" He stopped and looked at her. She was clearly agitated, but her voice

153

possessed a distinct giddiness.

Alan said, "Are we done here?"

"And you sound like him too!" she cried. Elise walked on ahead, and Alan followed her out of the restaurant, leaving our booth to process what had happened. "I'm so confused. I'm so confused!" she said.

Dad had figured it out. Talking to Alan face-to-face made the truth clear for him. He left the booth and went outside to talk to Alan.

"What is going on?" Mom said. "That's really not him?"

I didn't know what to say at that point. I wasn't sure whether or not the experiment was still going, so I just shook my head.

Alan and Dad returned, and I said, "It was Alan. We tricked you."

"But Alan's in Minnesota. He has that tournament today," Mom said.

"I decided not to do it," Alan said.

"So you're Alan?"

"Yep."

"Let me see your license. I want to be sure."

Ten minutes earlier, she couldn't believe Alan was not Alan, but after we revealed the truth, she couldn't believe he was. It appeared that once a person was convinced of a new reality it was difficult for the person to adjust back to the old reality. Once she saw Alan's license, though, she was on the path back to the comfortable familiarity of the old reality, and her world felt safe again.

The Answer

Given the right circumstances and careful preparation, a mother can speak directly to her son and be fooled into believing that it is not him.

Negotiating the Terms

They say you can tell a lot about a town by listening to its residents. If this is true, it's not good news for Beaumont, Texas.

It's a typical Sunday afternoon. I sit at a corner table at Bayou City Café with a stack of essays to grade, but the peaceful atmosphere doesn't last long. I have only made it through three essays when they sit down at the next table. The man is young and attractive, the woman middle-aged and a little lumpy. They each have a Bible, hers fairly tattered and his newer.

"It's like we talked about in church this morning. It's not real. It's satire," he says.

"What is satire? I know I've heard the word, but I don't know what it means," she says.

He pauses and starts, "Satire is like I'm talking to you, but I'm not really talking about you. It's like the layers of this cake." He pokes at the frosting with his fork. "There is sweetness and other flavors too."

"I think I know what you mean," she says and nods.

"Try this one. Who is Jesus?" he asks.

"Jesus is the son of God," she says but raises her voice at the end to make it a question.

"No! It doesn't say that in there," he says and slaps her Bible. "That is an illogical inference that people take from a misreading of the Bible. Are you Jesus?"

"No."

"Exactly, but he is in you, right?"

"Yes."

"Now you're getting it," he says. "What do you think about the

155

Catholics? Are they right?"

"They can live wherever they want to and believe in God," she says.

"That's all well and good, but the thing you have to understand is that they created this book in order to distribute it to the masses. They are like musicians who write to distribute themselves."

"I understand what you mean," she says.

"They were letting women become virgins. They were letting them have sex. It's like those seven candles . . . seven candlesticks listed in Revelations. They show the sins of the seven continents. Paul said, 'Do this, or I'm going to smite you.' With the death of John, there were no disciples left. Ten years later all the temples were destroyed. Christians were murdered for almost a hundred years. This is why we can't tolerate music. It comes from the same selfish, self-serving ideal. This is what happens," he says.

"But how do we get rid of it?" she asks.

"It starts with yourself. Remove it from your life. Then spread out. Spread out." He waves his arms wildly. "Go out to all the churches and explain what I'm telling you. We need to get rid of it. There are over five-thousand churches in the world using music. Start with them."

"Okay," she says and nods her head.

"Then double your strength for the unbelievers. Take the ones you've reached with you. It's what I'm working on."

"What do we do with the music?" she asks.

"Burn it. Burn it," he says, and I wonder if the Louis Armstrong song in the background is bothering him.

She smiles and nods.

"We can tell that music is corrupt. For example, five-hundred years ago there wasn't any music, and people were more pure then."

"That's a good point," she says.

"When we got away from Latin we started to only use music for evil. That took about eighty years."

"Wow," she says.

"After eighty years the word was no longer in a pure form. The Bible was stripped down to a bare level so the commoners could understand it, and the music got words . . . evil words."

"I see," she says.

"Then the army converted as many people as they could to Catholicism. They did this in the name of Christ. All those little churches said 'We're not doin' anything you say because your version is not what we saw.' Peter never left Jerusalem. They burned all the temples to the ground. It was kind of a slap in the face to the prophesy of Jesus. That's how I know that something bad is going to happen now, like Jerusalem will be blowed up."

"Wow. You think?"

"I know. It's all in there," he says and points to her Bible. He picks it up and says, "This is a good translation. You see what I'm saying? They make it into a cleaner and cleaner translation that it is so far removed from the 300 A.D. translation. Not to even get into the fact that it contradicts itself ten-thousand times. These two can't coexist because it cancels each other out. You see what I'm saying?"

"Yeah," she says and nods.

"The more I studied, the more I realized that the majority of the faith is like America, so far removed from the truth."

"Yeah."

"Even if you talked to Peter, who was only three sources removed from the truth, you would be deceived. They won't let you see Paul. They perverted the word of God. There is an entire book of Jesus locked in a vault somewhere in Europe that you don't ever get to read. I want to read that book, but the Catholics won't let you get a hold of it."

"Wow," she says.

"That's why everything corrupts over time. If you put money in a savings account you may believe it is growing, but really it is corrupting. The devil is changing that money over time. It's the ignorance of man who believes the change is a good thing."

"Interesting," she says, and I start to shift uncomfortably in my chair.

"You see all these people on TV talking about saving for retirement. They want you to think that way, but that's not what God wants. God wants us to trust that He will provide. If we trusted Him then we wouldn't have to buy into the evil system. We would know that when the money grows it is really the devil feeding it."

"That makes sense," she says.

"And it's more than that. Those people who are saving for retirement are doing it for pure selfish pleasure. It's like the homosexuals. They are acting out of lust because they want to ruin this country. They want to revert back to the time before the Bible was written."

"I see what you mean," she says.

"That's why, if you pay attention to what's happening, you'll notice that more and more musicians are homosexuals. Those two sins go together."

"Interesting."

"So many people have their own little solutions to these problems, but we need to band together. We need to get rid of all of it. The only way to get the homosexuals out of our country is to remove all the music. They can all go somewhere else. It's like the Bible says, remove the sin, and the sinner will follow."

"Where do you think they would go?" she asks.

"The thing is . . . it doesn't really matter. There are countries that aren't Christian. God created those places for a reason. They can go there," he says.

"So do I have to get rid of music that doesn't have words too?" she asks.

"Yes. Burn it all! All music was created in order to make people feel like God. They use it to control us. The only pure music is the music of the earth. If you want to hear music, listen to the river. Instruments are evil."

"Do you think homosexuals were the ones to invent the instruments?" she asks.

"It's very likely," he says, and I realize that I am no longer capable of listening to them without violently interfering in their private conversation, so I gather my things and relocate to a table in the back room.

* * *

I am alone momentarily, sitting at the new location with the stack of essays to look over. After just a few minutes, a couple walks in, disappears to order coffees, and sits down at the table across from me. She looks about twenty, is wearing black leggings over a hot pink top, has dark hair with a few golden strands in the front, and is thin all over with a pleasant face. He is probably in his sixties, wears the kind of jeans that are marketed to high school guys or young adults, and sports a tight black t-shirt to accentuate the fact that he obviously works out. He's short, but his cowboy boots add a little height and bring him eye to eye with his companion.

"I've been thinking about it, and I want a cat," she says.

"If you want a cat, I'll get you a cat. No problem." She smiles. "I'm really glad we're doing this. I thought about it a lot the last couple of days, and I know we're both going to benefit." She smiles but shifts uneasily in her chair. "We talked before about you being okay with this, but I want to briefly revisit that subject. It's important for me to know that you're okay with this. Is there anything that scares you?"

"No, I'm just still getting used to everything."

"Totally understandable," he says. "It's normal to feel that way. That's why I wanted to meet. I want to get everything ironed out before the wedding."

"Yeah, I know. You're right. It's a good idea to talk about it now," she says.

"What are some of your concerns?"

She pauses. "I hate cleaning. My parents always want the house clean and neat, but I'd rather be doing something else," she says and pulls her hair back into a ponytail.

"Oh, sweetie, no. Don't you worry about that. I have a cleaning service come every week. No pretty little wife of mine will have to clean the house."

She smiles and sits back, noticeably more relaxed. "I like that idea," she says.

"Another thing I want you to know is that I like shopping for you. A lot of people have a hard time believing that, I know, but I do. It's like I told you that night we met—it gives me pleasure to dress a beautiful woman."

"Yeah, I liked the clothes you bought me last time. Shoes are good too, and purses are good."

"That reminds me. I was gonna ask you about this. What is the big deal with the Louis Vuitton thing? I got no problem spending that kind of money. You know that. Like I told you, I got no problem spending two-thousand on clothes for you, but I'm just curious what the big deal is with these purses."

"I don't really know. It's just a status thing, I guess. I just like them," she says and shrugs her petite shoulders.

"I got you. I got you. By the way, winter's coming, and I want you to have a really nice coat, something stylish. Would you like that?"

"Sure. Why don't you just get me a gift card again?"

"Sure, or I could come with you," he says.

"You don't have to do that. I saw some nice ones at Dillard's."

"I'm on it, sweetie. I'll put a little extra on the card in case you want some shoes too."

"Thanks."

He scans the room, maybe searching for familiar faces, and says, "Let's talk a little about your allowance. Feels funny calling it that, but I guess that's what it is. What do you think is fair?" She shrugs her shoulders. "Okay, okay. I'll tell you what I was thinking . . . does six grand a month seem okay?"

She looks disappointed. "I guess so."

"Okay, okay. We'll make it seven." She smiles. "Now as far as travel is concerned, I like to go on several trips a year, some of them international. We'll have to get you a passport. Are you okay with being my travel companion?"

"Sure."

"I also want you to know that your parents will be taken care of. I don't want you to stress about their financial stuff anymore."

"Thanks."

"And, of course, if we happen to have children, they'll be taken care of too. I'll arrange everything."

"Okay," she says and takes out her phone. She appears to be typing out a text message. She puts the phone back into her pink purse and says, "Would it be okay if I went to college?"

"Sure, sure, of course, but let's leave it at that. I really don't want you working, sweetie. No, I wouldn't like that. It's better if you can just relax."

"I'm not arguing with that," she says.

"Also, I prefer a peaceful home. You know what I mean—no loud music, no crazy parties, that kind of thing. But you're not that kinda girl anyway, right?"

"No, not really," she says and giggles.

"And let's do the faithful thing, okay? I'm a pretty jealous guy, and my temper can be bad sometimes, so it'll be better that way." She looks at her phone again. "And if you do have to spend time with someone else . . . I guess things happen sometimes . . . but if you do, I don't want to know about it. You see what I'm saying? Keep it out of my sight."

"Okay."

"How are you doing with all of this? Is this going okay? Do you feel comfortable?" he asks.

"I'm kinda hungry. Would you get me some ice cream?" she asks.

"Sure, sweetie. What kind you want?"

"Get me some vanilla soft serve with strawberries on top."

"On my way," he says and disappears for a few minutes. I start to focus on my grading again, and he's back. "Here you go, sweetie," he says and hands her the small dish.

"Thanks." She takes a dainty bite of the soft serve.

"Now that you have your ice cream, I need to bring up the awkward thing," he says. She looks down and giggles. "This is something I should've straightened out with my ex-wife before we got married. It would've saved a lot of trouble." She keeps her eyes on the ice cream and slowly works her way through the dish. "I'm just gonna go ahead and say it. I'm a man. I need sex." I notice the older couple at the table on the other side of them has stopped talking, and it's comforting to not be the only eavesdropper. "I think twice a week is a decent expectation. What do you think?"

She shifts in her chair and says, "Sure. That should work."

"Okay, now that we got the awkwardness out of the way, where would you like to eat tonight? I know you need more than that little dish of ice cream."

"Harrison's was good. I really like their steak," she says.

"Then we'll do that again." He looks at his watch. "Do you want to go to the mall after?"

"Sure."

"We'll get you that coat. Would that be okay? I'd like to help you pick it out."

"Sure."

"And you're going to need a good one. I'm thinking about a trip to Banff this winter."

"Where?"

"It's in Canada. A real pretty town . . . mountains and skiing and all that."

"Cool," she says.

"Hmm . . . I wonder if we can get you a passport in time. I almost forgot about that. You need a passport for Canada now. Well . . . if we can't, we can always go to Colorado. Ever been there?"

"No," she says.

"You'll like it, sweetie. We'd stay at a real nice lodge with an indoor pool and hot tub. Now, that's real relaxation."

"Cool," she says.

"Are you just about done with that?" he says and nods toward the ice cream.

"Yeah, I don't really want the rest . . . now that I'm thinking about Harrison's."

"Yeah, me too . . . me too. It's nice to have a little something sweet, though," he says and playfully pinches her shoulder. They get up, he takes her dish over to the trash can, and then they are gone, out into the world beyond my earshot.

CPSIA information can be obtained at www.ICGtesting.com
Printed in the USA
BVOW02s1833300915

420343BV00002B/57/P